MCCRACKEN

AND THE

LOST LAGOON

Something moved through the waters, way above me. I turned to get a better view of it, wondering if it was some large sea creature, but what I saw instead was the narrow axe-head prow of a German U-boat. What looked like stubby wings were actually the fins that controlled the submarine's depth. I saw that it would pass directly overhead. A horrible thought occurred to me, and I gazed back along the slack arc of my lifeline, the air-hoses and steel cable that linked me to the surface of the ocean.

The slender prow of the U-boat brushed my lifeline. A tremor ran down its length that I could feel echoing in my suit. The lifeline slid down the side of the submarine until it reached the fin, where it lodged.

"Great Sc—!" I cried out. But the last syllable was cut short. The submarine passed overhead. I was jerked off my feet and flew through the murky water after it, keelhauled through the gloomy depths.

MCCRACKEN
AND THE
LOST LAGOON

By Mark Adderley

Scriptorium
Press
Yankton, South Dakota
2016

Published by Scriptorium Press,
Yankton, South Dakota

To Ellie

Contents

CHAPTER 1
A MEETING IN THE JUNGLE

I didn't have to be here, I reflected, as I watched the bandit emerge from the jungle at the far end of the bridge.

I could be at home—or what was home for the moment, anyway—in Belize City, with my beautiful wife Ariadne and our newborn son Archie.

Or perhaps I could be in Aberdeen, celebrating the Hogmanay, the Scottish New Year. But that had been a little over a fortnight ago, and it really didn't seem like New Year at all in the steaming, hot jungle. I missed the damp, the rain, the louring clouds of the land of my birth. I swatted a mosquito as another bandit stepped out of the dark forest and joined the first.

In fact, I thought, as the number of the bandits doubled once more, I would rather be almost anywhere than here, which was in central America, a hundred miles from the nearest city where anyone spoke English, where the cardinal rule for life was *Do what the cartels tell you.*

The jungle disgorged several more bandits, who joined the swelling group facing us across the top of the ravine. They were dressed in a more or less similar fashion, in dirty shirts and patched trousers that had once been white or pale blue, battered hats, strings of bullets crossed over their chests. A couple of them held sticks of bright orange dynamite; another bore a coil of fuse-wire over his shoulder and a plunger in one hand. The rest carried an assortment of rifles and shotguns, slung casually over their shoulders as if they were nothing more harmful than walking sticks.

Nevertheless, as they arrived at the far end of the bridge, they took up offensive positions behind trees or the bridge's anchor-posts. They raised their weapons in readiness, the muzzles gaping like hungry mouths. In the end, about a dozen of them stood or knelt on the far side of the bridge. On the near side, just me and José. Two of us left to guard the bridge until nightfall, when the detachment of British soldiers we had been promised would turn up.

Seeing all these bandits, José cleared his throat. He had been my guide and was now my good friend. Dark-complexioned, he had the chiseled features of his people. We had been in a number of scrapes together in the six months I'd been adventuring in the

10

British Honduras. And he was a good man to have around—I once saw him get a jaguar between the eyes with his throwing knife at forty feet, though he claimed it was more luck than accuracy.

"I do not think I like this, señor," said José. "Those *banditos*, there are very many of them."

"It's taken us two months to build that bridge," I replied. "I'm not going to let them just blow it up."

José made the Sign of the Cross, and started praying the *Paternoster*. I prayed with him, fixing the bandits with a wary eye as I recited the Latin words familiar from the Mass.

One of the bandits stepped onto the bridge. I fingered the retention strap on my holster. The bandit shouted across to us in Spanish. While he was talking, I leaned over the side of the bridge and spat into the roaring waters of the river it spanned. It took for ever to drop the sixty feet to the water, which foamed about the rocks below. If Ari had been here, she would have known what he was saying, and would probably have known a few choice insults to hurl back at him. Not for the first time, I regretted her absence. She could not accompany me on this expedition because she had just had a baby, whom I had seen for only a couple of days during a weekend's leave.

"Señor McCracken," said José urgently, breaking in on my reverie, "this *hombre*, he says this bridge will be bad for business."

I nodded. "Bad for *his* business, you mean. Now your villagers will be able to get to the markets in a day, not in three, and he won't be able to act as their broker." Their broker, I thought, who charged a very high percentage on all their goods, who made sure they were always poor and dependent. With the bridge, the villagers could get to the markets more quickly, and under the protection of the British police.

The bandit spoke again. José translated: "He says that you should turn around and walk away from the bridge. This is not a good place for you. If you stay, he says he will not be responsible for what happens next."

"Tell him I built the bridge, and I'll stay here and protect it for the villagers," I snapped back, and added, "Warn him, he crosses it at his own peril." José translated, and the bandit talked back. I knew what he would say—he would repeat that the bridge was bad for business.

A harsh laugh echoed across the ravine, and another bandit, who was a good bit wider in the girth than the others, stepped forward. He shoved past his spokesman. Shotgun slung over his shoulder, two huge knives and several throwing daggers thrust into his belt, his chin bristling with whiskers and a fat Havana cigar clenched between his teeth, he stood boldly, legs astride, on the bridge.

"Well, look at this," I said, very quietly, so as not to show my surprise. "I think this is the head *hombre* himself, Calavera." In the two months we had been building and guarding the bridge, Calavera had sent his men against us, but had never showed up himself. And now here he was, as large as life, twice as fat, and four times as ugly.

Calavera spoke in English. "Señor McCracken, be wise. Why do you want to help these miserable little villagers? They cannot do nothing but grow sugar cane and bananas. All I am doing is helping them to fulfill their . . . Hey, José, how do you say *potencial* in Gringo?"

"Potential?" suggested José.

"*Si, potencial,*" returned Calavera. "I am helping them to fulfill their *potencial*. Either they can scratch out a miserable living from the soil here in the jungle, or they can help Don Hernando Calavera del Armario—which is me—expand his empire. On the one hand, they can be a bunch of nobodies; on

13

the other, part of a machine that is destined for glory."

"Nobody likes machines more than I do, Calavera," I shouted back at him. "But I think they have a right to make their own living without being terrorized by crazy men who don't care if they live or die."

Calavera shrugged, puffed on his cigar, and said, "It's no different than your big industries in Europe—the industries that are making bigger and bigger machines to kill more and more soldiers."

I tried not to let on how deeply that one stung. It was true that the War was increasingly intense and violent back in Europe: more and more nations had entered the conflict, and the Germans had just, a few weeks ago, executed a nurse, whom they claimed was a spy. I said, "That's a different matter, Calavera. Here and now, what you're doing is wrong. And I'm going to stop you."

Calavera held up a hand. "There is nothing you can do to stop us, Señor McCracken, but I will permit you to leave this place with your lives, on one condition."

I cocked my head. "And that condition is what, exactly?"

"The gold you have discovered, the gold of the Mayans. Let me have it, and I will not kill you and your friend."

José's eyes widened. "How does he know about the gold, Señor McCracken?" he asked. There was a glint in his eye.

"How indeed?" I wondered. I shouted back to the bandit leader, "That gold is way north of here, in an underground cavern. There's none here."

Calavera sauntered a few yards further onto the bridge. "Come now, Señor McCracken. I know you have found Mayan gold here. Why else would you build this splendid bridge for these pathetic little *paletos*?"

I rested my hand on the grip of my revolver. "You've been misinformed, Calavera."

Calavera's lips widened into a grin. "I do not think so, señor. My informant is someone very close to you."

I turned to José. "You?"

"That is correct, señor!" cried José, backing away and stepping off the bridge. To Calavera he cried out: "Come across the *bridge, mi amigo*! I will show you where the gold is—remember *mi porcentaje*."

"Filthy traitor!" I roared, lunging after José. He ducked behind a great moss-covered rock, and I

15

leaped after him. I could hear cries of gold-lust and the tramping of boots on the wooden bridge behind me as the bandits dashed across it.

Behind the boulder, José's hand rested on a lever. He nodded; I nodded back grimly.

I peered around the side of the boulder. Most of the bandits were on the bridge. The last of them stepped onto it. "Now!" I shouted.

José threw the lever. A pulley quivered as the rope moved through it. A hook pulled on a catch on the under-side of the bridge. A trapdoor the length of the bridge swung downwards. In a split second, the exultant cries of the bandits turned to terror and dismay. They flung their arms wide. They hurled their rifles and shotguns aside. For a few seconds, they seemed suspended in mid-air, and then they plunged through the misty void towards the seething river below.

No one was left on the bridge.

"I wish they could have seen reason," I said, my stomach queasy.

"It is a shame," agreed José. "But if they had, it would have been the first time in many years—since I have known them. *Gracias*, Señor McCracken," he added. "Now my village can live in peace, and prosper." He reached into the ferns to reveal a crank, a bit like a ship's helm. He gave it a few turns and, under the bridge, a telescopic arm extended, pushing the trapdoor slowly back into its place.

"You were very convincing, José," I said. "I almost believed you'd betrayed me. You should consider a career in acting."

"Señor McCracken," said José soberly, "I would never betray you. You owe me too many tequilas."

Suddenly, his eyes widened and his lips pulled back from his teeth. His right hand clutched across his chest.

The hilt of a dagger protruded from his left shoulder.

I spun round. To my horror, I saw that Calavera had survived. Being closer to the bank, he had not fallen quite so far as the others, and had landed in the soft ferns. I closed in and grappled with him. He balled his fist and struck me in the face. Pain exploded in my cheek, but I didn't let him go. I pulled on him, struggling to bring him to the ground. He reeked of tequila and cigars, and he remained stubbornly upright. I lashed out with my foot, swiping at his legs, but he dodged—he was quicker than I expected. He wrapped his foot around my leg, and I felt my knees give way.

With a shout, I dropped from the side of the ravine. But I wasn't alone—Calavera tumbled with me. We bounced through ferns and palmettos, rolling, our arms and legs flailing. Finally, we came to a rest on a wide, grassy delta, past which the river roared. We were both shaken, and struggled only slowly to our feet. The delta was fringed with shallow rock-pools and pock-marked all over with little grey hills. The body of one of the bandits lay, his arms and legs at weird angles, about ten feet from me.

He seemed to be moving, but as I stared at him, I saw that something was moving on him, and then I knew what the little grey mounds were.

They were red fire ant mounds. The red fire ant, that could strip a beast to the bones in minutes.

But I couldn't reflect on this because Calavera was on his feet, a wicked-looking knife in his hand, which he whirled this way and that, grinning over the flashing silver of the blade.

I reached to my hip and drew my revolver, my thumb on the hammer as I raised it.

Calavera's hand flashed out and there came a metallic *Ding!* sound as his knife hit my revolver. For a moment, I saw the pistol flying through the air.

Then it landed with a thud in the middle of one of the ant mounds.

I like the gun, I thought, but not that much.

"Give up, *Gringo*," snarled Calavera. "It is too hot to be fighting."

"You give up first," I told him. I ran at him and he thrust his knife at me. But I pummeled aside his knife-hand. My attack drove him back a little way. His feet slithered to a stop just inches from one of the ant-mounds, but then he regained control of himself and pushed back against me. I took a step back, but he had extended too far, and I took the advantage, launching my knee up into the soft flesh beneath his ribcage. He leaped away, clutching his stomach, dancing this way and that to avoid the ant-mounds. I was after him in a moment, but he kicked at my ankles and I fell on my side with a thud that drove the breath from my lungs.

My face was just a few inches from the grimacing face of the dead bandit. Fire-ants, some of them an inch long, swarmed over his back. I could hear their jaws and legs clicking faintly, beneath the roaring of the river.

Calavera cackled with laughter. He grabbed my hair and pushed my face towards the ants. I strained

19

against him, but he had the advantage of height and weight, and I knew I could not resist long.

"*Buenas noches*, Señor McCracken," said Calavera. "Be a nice meal."

But then he gave a sharp cry and released me. I squirmed around to look. Blood trickled down the side of his face—something had hit him in the head. I wrenched myself from under him and leaped to my feet. He struggled upright, shaking his head. On the ground nearby lay a knife. I stole a glance upwards. José stood at the top of the ravine, his hand clutching his wound.

"More luck than accuracy, Señor McCracken!" he cried out.

Probably—and he had only distracted Calavera for a moment, not incapacitated him. But I drove my fist up into his stomach, where I had hit him before, and with a grunt he stepped backwards.

Right onto an ant-mound.

In his terror, he spun away from the swarm of little red devils and overbalanced. He fell over a slick rock and into the shallows beyond. I followed him, fists at the ready. For a few moments, we traded blows, neither of us moving backwards or forwards. I circled about in an effort to find a good opening, but found none; and now, my back was to the raging river. I could feel the cool spray over my back.

Calavera was impatient. With a howl of rage, he rushed at me. I dropped to one knee and, when he was close, shoved him upwards, my biceps screaming a protest, so that his momentum carried him, spiraling, over my head. With a terrible *splat!* and a bit of a *crunch!* he landed behind me. I spun round. He lay among the rocks at the very edge of the shallows, but from the waist down he was actually immersed in the river, which foamed white all about him. His fingers scrabbled at the slick rocks, and I knew he could not hold on much longer.

For a moment, while time seemed suspended, a debate raged in my soul. I wanted very much to let him be swept away to his death. I watched his fingers clutching, his eyes widening. I thought of the poor villagers he'd terrorized for ten years, of the profit he'd made from their poverty. What could be more fitting than to see him engulfed by the river?

But that wasn't my job, I knew.

I dashed forward and bent down to help him. But when my hands were close to his, he let go of the rock and seized my wrists in a powerful grasp.

"You and me," he sneered, "we go together, *Gringo!*"

21

His dark eyes flashed as his fingers tightened their grip.

Fear crawled in my gut. He's going to take me with him, I thought, panic rising in me. God help me!

The river drew the bandit into its embrace, and he dragged me with him. I dug in my heels, the rocks hard and slippery against the soles of my boots, and I could get no traction. I thrust my shoulder against one rock, ground my knee against another, but the waters, cool and remorseless, foamed over Calavera, and halfway up my leg. My foot slipped, then my shoulder. I slid deeper into the water, and deeper still.

Then, with a lurch, the bandit's fingers slid off my wrists and with a curse he released me. For a moment, I glimpsed his face, snarling with anger; and then he was gone, and only the rapids remained. Slowly, in a daze, I got to my feet.

It took me quite a while to climb back up the side of the ravine, and when I finally got to the top, I found José, as I might have expected, surrounded by pretty villagers who were binding up his wound.

Sixty feet below, the river seethed away, carrying with it the menace that had hung over the village for almost a decade.

CHAPTER 2
A CHANCE TO GO HOME

His Majesty's Government had kindly provided us with a neat little stucco house in Belize City, pale tangerine in colour, with a terracotta roof and white window frames. A single palm tree stood in the tiny garden, where its fronds cascaded over the white-painted iron fence. I had probably spent three weeks in it during the six months we had lived in the British Honduras.

After I had made the long trek back from the jungle, Ari kindly let me sleep in late, and when I awoke it was to find Archie already alert and staring at his surroundings, kicking his tiny feet and wagging his hands with enthusiasm. Ari joined me beside the crib, and we spent a few moments marveling at the splendour of God's creation. I reached into the crib, picked him up, and placed him against my shoulder, where he could nuzzle his soft little cheek against me. I kissed the downy dark fuzz on the top of his head.

"It's good to have you back," Ari said, as we left the nursery for the dining room. At the smell of eggs and sausages, my stomach growled with anticipation.

"Breakfast is served in the *Speiseraum*." Fritz stood at attention in the dining room—he invariably called it the *Speiseraum*. Our loyal servant, red-haired and wall-eyed, was probably the best cook in the world, and I'm not exaggerating. "May I take *die Knabe* McCracken?" he asked, holding out his hands. I reluctantly handed Archie over to him, but enthusiastically sat down to sausages and eggs.

Fritz can make anything in the realm of food. He can taste something from the Himalayas once and then reproduce it months later in London, or New York, or Belize City. He can create meals that are culinary masterpieces on a level with Michelangelo's David or Leonardo's Mona Lisa. And he chooses to stay with us! It's one of God's great blessings.

"Have Archie and Fritz been getting along well?" I asked, spreading the napkin on my knee and reaching for a piece of lightly-browned toast.

"Archie loves him!" Ari carefully spread butter to the very edges of her toast. "Fritz can almost always calm him down when he's upset." She drew a deep breath. "Still, it would be great to have a nurse."

25

I nodded. "I'll see if I can find one today. Maybe the Governor will know of someone."

"When is your appointment?"

I looked at my watch. "In about two hours," I said. "Mmm—did Fritz make this jam? It's delicious. What is it?"

"Mango," answered Ari, taking some for herself.

We ate in appreciative silence for a few moments. "I hope the Governor doesn't want me to build another bridge," I said at last. "I'm tired of adventuring. I thought the incident with the Garifuna Indians was enough, but then came that chase through the jungle with the bicycles and the macaws, and now this business with the bridge and the bandits. I'd like to settle down and live a quiet life for a while."

"Nice timing," observed Ari, with an ironic smile, "in the middle of a war."

"Did you read this letter from England?" I held up an envelope.

"No, it was addressed to you."

"It's a job offer. Remember that chap we met last time we were in England?"

"Gilbert Chesterton?"

"No, the other one—the engineer from Vickers Armstrong, the aeroplane manufacturers. Barnes

Wallis is his name. Anyway, they're looking for someone to help design bombs and navigation systems for aeroplanes, and Wallis thought of me."

"So you'd rather make bombs than have adventures?" Ari wrinkled her perfect brow.

"Well, there's Archie to think about as well," I pointed out. "Adventuring is no life for a baby. And what if I get killed? I nearly did with that jaguar. Only José's accuracy and luck saved me."

Ari shrugged. "The accuracy and luck were there when you needed them." She smiled, reached across the table, and squeezed my hand. "Really, though, can you imagine life without adventure? You?"

"I know, it's hard to imagine what you've never had." I tried one of the sausages. The skin burst, releasing a delicious combination of rosemary, sage, thyme, and peppers as it did so. "But I think I could do it. I think I could enjoy a quiet life."

Ari sliced one of the sausages with her knife, popped a piece into her mouth, and chewed thoughtfully a moment before swallowing. She set aside her fork. "So, let me get this straight. You, McCracken the Engineer, discoverer of lost civilizations and scourge of villains all over the world, would get up at seven in the morning, eat a quick

27

breakfast, kiss me and Archie goodbye, then get on a train to ride to Vickers Armstrong, make bombs all day (with a lunch hour at noon and a midmorning and midafternoon break), then come home at five to read the newspaper before supper."

"Dinner. We'd call it dinner back home."

"Dinner," agreed Ari. "Which newspaper would you prefer? The *Times*? The *Telegraph*?"

"You're mocking me, aren't you?" I wrinkled my nose at her.

"Well, I know you very well," she replied.

An hour and a half later, the late morning sun blazed down upon me as I walked towards Government House. I turned at the gate, nodding a greeting to Perkins, the sentry of the day, and striding up through the neatly-kept lawns and flower-beds tended by several local gardeners.

The Governor's secretary, the pretty, round-faced Miss Montero, met me at the door and led me up the stairs towards the Governor's office.

"You don't have to come with me," I said. "I know the way."

Miss Montero flashed a smile, her bobbed hair swaying as she did so. "Someone must take notes, señor," she said. She knocked smartly on the Governor's door, then pushed it open for me.

The Governor of the British Honduras, a grey-haired man in his early sixties, went by the name of William Collett. He rose from the chair behind his wide teak desk and invited me to sit down opposite him.

"How are Mrs. McCracken and the baby?" he asked.

"Both doing very well," I replied, "thank you."

"Miss Montero," said Collett, "would you mix Mr. McCracken and myself a couple of refrescos, please?" The secretary stood and moved over to the drinks cabinet. "Do you and Mrs. McCracken have everything you need?" asked Collett.

"Ari was thinking we might employ a nurse," I said. "If you could recommend someone, I'd be obliged."

"Let me think about it," answered Collett. "I'll ask around, or have Miss Montero do that for me. Thank you, my dear," he added, taking the refresco she offered him. I sipped mine, a refreshing combination of mangoes and pineapple that cooled me to the core on the hot day.

Collett, meanwhile, had slid open a drawer and taken out a black velvet bag. "About six months ago," he said, "right after that unpleasant business with the U-boat and Professor Lychfield, you gave us some very valuable information about where we might find some sunken treasure. I wanted you to know that your information was spot-on." Pulling the strings of the velvet bag, he revealed a golden figurine, about eight inches in height, of someone who appeared to be dancing. He wore a fantastic headdress, which consisted largely of feathers, and carried a snake in his hands.

"Is it Kinich Ahau?" I asked, remembering the name of a Mayan idol from our adventures in Mexico.

"I'm sure I have no idea," replied Collett. "From the point of view of His Majesty's Government, it's gold, saleable gold. Our boys on the Western Front can continue the good fight, confident their pay will turn up on time, and we can continue manufacturing rifles and bullets. The war against the Kaiser's tyranny can continue, thanks to you." Collett drew the velvet back up over the Mayan idol's head and replaced it in his drawer. "This, together with some other items we've recovered, will reside in our vaults until they can be sold. Well done, McCracken—well done indeed." He paused. "Just one more treasure," he said, reaching again into his desk. This time, he handed me an envelope, made of heavy paper, sealed with red wax.

Frowning, I broke the seal, drew out the stiff paper, and read the following words:

George the Fifth, by the Grace of God of the United Kingdom and Ireland and of the Dominions Beyond the Seas King, Defender of the Faith, Emperor of India, and Sovereign of the Most Honourable Order of the Bath, to McCracken, Engineer and Adventurer, greeting.

Whereas we have thought it fit to nominate and appoint you to be an Honourary Member of the Civil Division of the Third Class or Companions of our said Most Honourable Order of the Bath, we do by these presents grant unto you the dignity of a Companion of the said Order and hereby authorize you to have, hold, and enjoy the said dignity and rank as an Honourary Member of the Civil Division of the aforesaid Order, together with all and singular privileges thereunto belonging and appertaining.

Given at our court of Saint James, under the sign manual and the Seal of our said Order, this twenty-second day of November, 1915, in the sixth year of our reign.

By the Sovereign's Command,

George, Grand Master.

"I don't understand," I said. "What does all that mean?"

"Please stand up," said Collett, and I did so. He stepped around the desk. He held a wide red ribbon upon which hung what looked like a gold medallion. "As the legal representative of His Britannic Majesty, George V, in the crown colony of the British Honduras," he said, "and as a Knight Commander of the Bath, I hereby invest you, McCracken, with all the rights and privileges appertaining to a Companion Member of the Civil Division of the Honourable Order of the Bath." He draped the medal about my shoulders and shook my hand. "Congratulations, McCracken," he said. "What does it mean? It means that, for your invaluable services to the Crown, you're now a Knight of the Bath." He grinned as he resumed his seat. "You can go on a quest, if you like."

I dropped into my own seat like a sack of coal. "I think I'm done with quests," I commented. "Well, what do I do now?" I asked.

"I suggest you go home and celebrate with your lovely wife, and . . . I believe the word is *bairn*?" I nodded. "Congratulations once more, McCracken—

a well-deserved honour!" I couldn't think of anything to say; I was too stunned. "The—ah—other thing I wanted to talk to you about can wait until tomorrow. I'd like you to meet someone from the French Embassy. I thought he'd be here today, but he seems to have been delayed. Shall we say, ten o'clock?

"I'll be here," I mumbled as I made my way, guided by Miss Montero, out of the Governor's office.

"Señor McCracken," said Miss Montero, as we reached the lobby, "you say you have need of a nurse?"

I nodded. "I do."

"My sister Assumpta has need of work," Miss Montero explained. "She lives in this city. She is very good with children. Perhaps I should suggest to her than she can call on your wife this afternoon?

"Thank you, Miss Montero," I said. "I'm sure Mrs. McCracken will be delighted to meet your sister."

I was halfway home before I realized that passersby were staring strangely at me because I hadn't thought to take off my medal yet. Hurriedly stuffing it into my pocket, I finished my walk home.

Ari beamed with delight at the prospect of getting a nurse. "Perhaps the next time there's any kind of adventure, we can go along together," she suggested.

"You think adventuring is a family activity?" I said in surprise.

"It's a McCracken family activity," Ari pointed out.

"But . . . well, it's dangerous."

"I know," replied Ari. "You said that this morning, and I knew it already—I've been on a lot of your adventures with you, dear, if you remember. But Archie has to learn somehow."

"He's a bit young for all that, don't you think?" Ari didn't answer in words, but I could tell from her expression that she didn't think much of my observations. Hurriedly, I added, "Well, we can talk about that *if* there's another adventure."

"Isn't that what the Governor wanted to talk to you about?" wondered Ari.

"What? Oh no, I almost forgot." I reached into my pocket and handed her the medal. "I got this, for finding all that treasure in Hoolie-Coolie-whatever-it-was-called last year."

"Xulamqamtun." Ari's pronunciation of the Mayan word was, as always, perfect. "What is this?"

34

"It's the Order of the Bath." I passed her the king's letter, a little crumpled now from my pocket. "I've been made a Knight of the Bath, with all the rights and privileges appertaining thereunto."

"Order of the Bath?" Ari turned the medal over in her hands and held it up to the light. "*Tria juncta in una*," she read. "Three joined in one? I wonder what that means. It sounds like the Blessed Trinity, but that can't be right."

"It probably means England, Ireland, and Scotland are joined in one nation, the United Kingdom of Britain," I suggested.

"Without Wales? That seems unfair—and rude, too. What are the rights and privileges appertaining thereunto?"

"I can call myself Sir McCracken, CB, and you can call yourself Ariadne, Lady McCracken."

"I kind of called myself that already," Ari pointed out. "Anything else?"

"Well, I get to use supporters on my coat of arms, and a band with the Order's motto all around it."

"Supporters? You mean, animals that hold the shield up?" I nodded. "But you don't have a coat of arms."

35

"Well, I'll get one," I said. "It can't cost much nowadays, and I bet there was a McCracken in the Middle Ages who went on a Crusade or something. Oh, and the Governor wants to see me tomorrow as well."

Ari looked relieved. "Perhaps there's another adventure for us," she suggested.

At that moment, Fritz opened the door of the parlour to announce that there was a lady wishing to see Frau McCracken about the position of Nurse. It was remarkable how similar to Miss Montero Assumpta was, other than the glasses and light hair. After shaking her hand, I went upstairs to read Brown's *507 Mechanical Movements* while the ladies talked. After some time had passed, I heard Archie stirring and, thinking Ari wouldn't want to be interrupted, I put Brown aside and sped to the nursery.

Assumpta was already there, cradling Archie in her arms, singing softly a lullaby in Spanish. I looked over at Ari.

"She's a real jewel," she said.

The next morning, I rose early, leaving Ari and Archie in bed, and ate an excellent breakfast of bacon, eggs, tomatoes, and fry jacks, which are lightly-fried triangles of dough, a little like doughnuts, drizzled with honey. By nine-thirty, I was out of the house and on the street.

Much was stirring at Government House when I pushed open the door and entered the lobby. People dashed back and forth, anxiety printed on their features. Collett was talking to a pair of white-uniformed policemen in pith-helmets.

"Oh, McCracken!" lamented Collett. "It's gone, it's gone—stolen in the night from our vaults."

"What's gone?" I asked.

"The golden statue—the one I showed you yesterday."

"Someone stole the idol!" I exclaimed. "Any clues? Did they take anything else?"

"As far as we can tell," said one of the pith-helmeted policemen, his voice deep and resonant, "the golden figure is the only thing missing. Did you see the item, sir? Could you give any further details about its appearance?"

I described what I could remember of the figurine, but could add little to what Collett had already told the police officer.

"The vault was closed when we got here this morning," Collett explained, "but it was . . . sealed." I raised my eyebrows, and Collett went on, "Sealed like a letter, with red sealing-wax, on which was impressed the image of a dragon and the words *The Jewel*."

"A dragon?" I was thinking hard. "In old stories, dragons like to hoard treasure."

"We don't know what the serpent means, but The Jewel is his name," said the policeman. "Not his real name, of course, but a kind of codename. He is an international jewel thief, and has struck at least twice before, once in San Francisco, and once in Buenos Aires. He always leaves the crime scene sealed with red wax, impressed with the dragon and his codename. And he always steals a single item, ignoring piles of other valuables, as in this case. Unfortunately, no one has ever seen him, so we have no description and no clues."

"I'm sorry to hear this, Collett," I said. "Shall I come back another time?"

"No, no, no," replied the Governor. "Auzepy is here already. Is there anything else, officer?"

"I think we have everything we need," replied the policeman and, with a smart salute, he and his partner turned and marched out of Government House.

"And to make things worse, Miss Montero has the day off today," said Collett, leading me up the stairs. A pair of gentlemen waited in his office, one

38

in his late fifties, the other a young man with a moustache. The older man turned to the younger and spoke a few words in French, and the young man left, nodding a greeting to me and Collett as he left.

"McCracken, may I introduce Pierre Auzepy, the French ambassador to Guatemala. Pierre, this is McCracken, the engineer."

"I am much delighted to make your acquaintance, Monsieur McCracken," said Auzepy, shaking my hand. "And may I offer you my congratulations on your nomination to the *Ordre de la Bain*."

I thanked him, and we dropped into wicker chairs about the cold fireplace. An awkward silence settled upon us. Collett hadn't even sent out for refrescos, which showed just how agitated he was. At last, he said, "Well, McCracken, I've had some bad news this morning, as you know. And I'm afraid it's my sad duty to deliver some bad news to you also."

"Bad news?" I sat up a little straighter.

"Yes, it concerns a friend of yours, Nicolas Jaubert."

Jaubert was one of my best friends, an expert diver and undersea explorer. I was beginning to be concerned. "What about Jaubert? I haven't seen

39

him since the time we were in New York together, last May."

"It seems, Monsieur McCracken," said Auzepy, "that Monsieur Jaubert, whilst working on a secret project for the French Navy off the coast of Cameroon, in West Africa, was involved in an explosion that sank his ship, the *Voltigeur*. Our efforts to find him have all failed, and at this point we must assume that he is dead."

CHAPTER 3
HMS HAM AND TRIPE

Silence fell upon the room. Collett wore a pained expression on his face; Auzepy merely looked sad. I felt as if my insides had been kicked out.

I made the Sign of the Cross. "Jaubert is dead?" My voice squeaked rather more than I liked.

"I am desperately sorry, monsieur," replied the French ambassador. "We know that you and Jaubert were close friends, and had worked together many times, but we can draw no other conclusion. It has now been more than five months since the disaster."

"Five months!" I exploded. "Why did no one tell me in all that time?"

Collett spread his hands sympathetically. "No one thought to, and communications are always so poor, especially in wartime. But as soon as the Prime Minister heard of the death of Mr. Jaubert, he wanted you specifically to know."

"Monsieur Jaubert," said Auzepy, "was working on a top secret undersea device when he was killed. We would like you to salvage the machine from the wreckage of the *Voltigeur*."

41

I gave an ironic smile. "An adventure," I said. I thought of Archie and Ari and our little house in Belize City; but I thought also of my friend, the wiry little Frenchman with a taste for Cognac and a passion for the sea. "What device was this?" I asked with a sigh.

Auzepy snapped open the locks of his briefcase and threw up the lid. He took out a large piece of paper and spread it out on Collett's desk. It was the blueprint of a very odd-looking vehicle.

"Is it a submarine?" I asked, puzzled. "Are those caterpillar tracks?"

"This, Monsieur McCracken, is the Corkindrill," announced Auzepy, not without a trace of pride. "It utilizes and combines the new technologies of submersible vessels and tanks, to produce a small two-man craft capable of sailing under the sea or over the land with equal facility. Jaubert was working on this with Capitaine Maurice Strombourg of the Marine Nationale."

"I've heard of Captain Strombourg," I said.

"He is a national hero," replied Auzepy.

"He rescued *HMS Dwarf* from enemy artillery in the Wouri Estuary of Cameroon late in '14," Collett reminded me. "Nearly eighty British sailors were saved by Strombourg's courage."

"He was awarded the *Légion d'honneur* for his bravery," interjected Auzepy. "Regrettably, Capitaine Strombourg also was killed by the explosion that killed Jaubert."

"Does anyone know what caused the explosion?" I asked.

"Most likely," said Auzepy, "it was a torpedo from a German U-boat. There have been many U-boat sightings in the waters of West Africa."

"Any survivors?"

"They were picked up by the Royal Navy," said Auzepy, "but Capitaine Strombourg and Jaubert were the only missing crewmembers."

"Is it possible they were in the Corkindrill, and not on the ship?" I asked.

"If that is the case, then where are they?" Auzepy shrugged. "We have to be certain that either the Corkindrill is destroyed or salvaged."

"You can see the strategic purpose of the Corkindrill, McCracken." Collett leaned back in the wicker chair and pressed his fingertips together. "Sailing down the Rhine or Danube, a fleet of Corkindrills could disable all the major German centres of industry. If the prototype were to fall into enemy hands, the position would be reversed." He paused, then asked anxiously, "Will you take the mission, McCracken?"

I didn't answer at once. Outside, the birds were singing and the sky was a vivid blue. I said slowly, "I thought I'd be giving up adventuring."

"You? Give up adventuring?" Collett's eyes were wide with surprise. "I'm sorry, McCracken, I'd just never thought you were the type for a quiet life."

"I have a family now," I observed.

"Well, of course. But you could take them with you. Hasn't your wife accompanied you on several of your adventures in the past?"

"She has. But the baby makes it all different." I sighed. "All right, Collett, one more adventure—for Jaubert. It's the least I can do for my old friend."

"Bravo, monsieur!" exclaimed Auzepy. Slipping the Corkindrill plans into a manila folder, he went on, "*Merci beaucoup.* I shall rest more easily knowing you are on the case."

"Report for duty aboard *HMS Amphitrite* tomorrow morning at 6:00 a.m.," said Collett. "Captain Evans has orders to convey you to Cameroon and to assist with salvage operations."

"Aye aye, sir," I said, and left his office.

I walked slowly home, my mind full of little things, of moments shared with Jaubert, his ancestral home in Brittany, the humorous glint in his eye before he did anything dangerous, the keen perception with which he had predicted the outbreak of war more than a year before it had happened, the passion with which he talked of sharks or squids or yachts or diving bells. Making the Sign of the Cross, I prayed for his soul and pushed open the front door of the little stucco house.

Ari cried, of course, and that made me cry too. We clung to each other in our grief, and each made wet the shoulder of the other.

"Five months!" said Ari, her face muffled by my shoulder. "Dead for five months, and we knew nothing!"

"My love," I said, "we're in the middle of the most devastating war in history, and this is most people's experience of it—there's hardly a woman or man in England who hasn't lost someone close."

"I'm sure you're right," said Ari, crossing herself, "but I can't help thinking of Nicolas in Thera, or New York. He saved my life in New York."

"He was a great man," I said, "and a great friend. Now it's up to us to make sure he didn't die in vain."

Ari smiled through the tears. "So now you want to go on an adventure?"

I nodded. "Just this once—for Jaubert."

Ari wiped her eyes. "Well, I guess I'd better help Fritz with the packing." She rose and left the room.

I stared through the window at the street outside. Horses and carts clattered past, and the occasional motor-car rattled over the cobblestones.

Across the road, my eyes clicked with someone who stood still, facing our house. He was young and moustached, and I knew I'd seen him, though I couldn't remember where. He crossed the street, turned, and strode away, and then I remembered that he had been with Auzepy in the Governor's office that morning. It was a curious coincidence that he should be here.

The following morning, a pair of soldiers turned up at our house and packed all our cases into a horse-drawn carriage. I climbed up next to Fritz, and Ari and Assumpta sat in the back with Archie, who was a little annoyed at waking up before he was quite ready. Fritz cracked the whip over the horses' backs and the carriage jolted away towards the docks.

We soon transferred ourselves to a motor-launch that puttered towards *HMS Amphitrite* on the waters of the bay before us.

"A fine ship," I told the sailor in the sternsheets, whose hand held the rudder.

"She's a good girl, the old *Ham-and-Tripe*," replied the sailor. At my raised eyebrow, he went on, "Sorry, sir, *Ham-and-Tripe* is the haffecionate term the members of the crew use for the old girl. It's a sort of salute to the galley crew, on haccount of the fine cuisine what they feeds us to keep our spirits up, when we is sailing about the world's oceans on His Majesty's business, Gawd save 'im."

"Why is she painted that way?" asked Ari. The *Amphitrite* bore odd stripes and blocks of white and blue and grey.

"It's called razzle-dazzle, ma'am," said the sailor. "It's camy-something."

"Camouflage?" suggested Ari.

"Aye, that would be hit, ma'am, camouflage. It don't make the old *Ham-and-Tripe* disappear, but it makes it 'ard for the 'Un to guess 'er range and size."

We hove to alongside the cruiser and, when the sailor had secured the launch fore and aft, we climbed aboard. A petty officer named Benson led us through a hatch and along a corridor lit by caged electric light-bulbs. The smell of oil and steel was extremely pleasant, like coming home after a long journey. I had introduced Archie, who was more himself now, to many nautical terms, such as *bulkhead*, *scuttle* and *companionway*, by the time we

47

reached the tiny cabin with a single porthole that would be our home for the voyage to Cameroon.

"Shall I unpack the suitcases now, Herr McCracken?" asked Fritz.

Before I could reply, Benson had made a startled movement. "Is there a problem, Benson?" I asked.

"Your man, sir," stammered the petty officer, "he's a H . . . a German."

"Very observant, Benson," I replied. "Fritz has been working for me since before hostilities began. He hasn't seen his family or set foot in Germany in all that time. He's my good friend, and loyal to His Majesty. Isn't that right, Fritz?"

"*Jawohl* . . . I mean, yes, Herr McCracken, that is correct," answered Fritz.

"Sorry, sir, I meant no disrespect," said Benson. "It's just that, most times we see Jerry, he's shooting at us."

I nodded. "And Fritz is an excellent shot with a pistol," I said. "But he's only ever fired on His Majesty's enemies."

"I see, sir," said Benson. "I'll pass the word round. The men . . . they might be a little . . . *prejudiced*, sir."

"I understand, Benson," I said. "Thank you for your concern and your help. You know, Fritz can help out on the voyage. He's also an excellent cook. You might put him to work in the galley?" I winked at Fritz, who winked back with one of those weird eyes of his.

"An excellent idea, sir. I'll talk to Cook. Mr. McCracken, should you have a moment's leisure after we set sail, Captain Evans would very much like to greet you himself. You'll find him on the bridge." And saluting smartly, Benson was gone to show Assumpta to her cabin.

Shortly afterwards, I heard the familiar throb of the engines pulsing up through the deck. As the *Amphitrite* turned slowly eastwards, Belize City slid out of the porthole. Archie looked up from Ari's arms, blew a raspberry, and wagged a plump little hand, as if saying goodbye.

Our journey to Africa had begun.

Captain Evans was a Welshman, a little shorter than me, with a face darkened and seamed by salt breezes and equatorial suns, his hair shot through with grey. He clasped my hand in a firm grip, more seams appearing about his eyes as he greeted me.

"A pleasure to have you on board, McCracken. I've heard so much about your . . . exploits."

"I'm sure some of it was true," I replied. "It's a lovely ship you have here."

Captain Evans beamed, looking with pride about the bridge. All was gleaming steel and brass and polished wood. "She's a grand old girl, the *Amphitrite*," he said proudly. "They don't make the protected cruisers any more—it's all light cruisers and battleships now. But the *Amphitrite* will serve her King and Country valiantly when the time comes. She can make over twenty-four knots if we push her a little. Normal cruising speed is about eighteen or nineteen."

"So," I said, performing a few mental calculations, "we should reach Cameroon in ten days?"

"Spot on, McCracken," said Evans, pulling around a chart and pointing to a course that took us across the Atlantic, from the Caribbean to the Gulf of Guinea.

After I had spent about an hour with Captain Evans on the bridge, soaking in the lovely efficiency of the Royal Navy and letting the muted gush of the sea and the tolling of the Engine Order Telegraph's bell calm my senses, I asked permission to explore the ship a little. I was about to leave, when Benson entered, carrying a covered tray.

"Compliments of Mr. Bauer, sir," Benson announced, pulling away the cover to reveal a delicious aroma of bacon, sausages, and tangy seafood. Beside the sausages and eggs lay shiny mounds of cockles and onions, and a small bowl of green spread. Captain Evans' eyes sprang open in surprise.

"Upon my soul!" he exclaimed. "Penclawdd cockles and *bara lawr!*"

"Bara what, sir?" wondered Benson.

"*Bara lawr*, man!" returned the Captain. "Laverbread—a Welsh delicacy, look you." Eagerly, he spread some of it lavishly onto a piece of toast and took a rapturous bite. "My word," he said, "the last time I ate *bara lawr* was in a little pub on the Mumbles, before the War. Do we have a Welshman working in the galley, Mr. Benson, and I wasn't informed?"

"No, sir," replied Benson. "This bara . . . this breakfast was prepared by a German, by Mr. Bauer, McCracken's man."

"By a German, no less?" Evans mused on the fact for a moment, then took another slice of toast and laverbread. "Well, wonders will never cease, Mr. Benson, Mr. McCracken, wonders will never cease." He had a dreamy expression on his face as he chewed thoughtfully on the laverbread. "I feel like I'm seven years old again! Come on, all you *Saeson*," he added to the bridge crew. "One at a time, now, don't abandon your posts. Come and try some real

51

food here. See how a real man eats breakfast, if you think your English stomachs are up to it!" Turning to Benson, he said, "Mr. Benson, please tell Mr. Bauer, *Diolch yn fawr.*"

"Sir?"

"Thank you very much."

Grinning with satisfaction, I made my exit from the bridge and went to explore the main deck. After wandering about for a bit and admiring the gleaming tubes of the great guns, the smell of the oil, steel and salt water, I found myself on the quarterdeck. Oddly enough, there wasn't another person in sight, just a crowd of air vents, like very still penguins. I leaned on the stern railing and watched the creamy wake frothing out behind us.

It was then that I heard the last thing I expected to hear on a Royal Navy ship: a French voice. And it said perhaps the last thing I expected to hear at that moment.

"Monsieur McCracken," it said, "would you please turn around slowly, and raise your hands above your head, or else I will blow a hole in your spine."

Turning slowly and raising my hands, I saw the last person I expected to see at that moment: the young Frenchman with the moustache from Government House, who had been standing outside my house in Belize City the previous day.

The Luger, though, I totally expected.

My eyes darted left and right about the ship. There was no one around—highly unusual on a crowded naval vessel like the *Amphitrite.* The barrels of three guns stared with empty menace at me, for behind Moustache stood the three-pounder stern guns, silent and unmanned now.

"What do you want with me?" I asked.

"It is very simple, Monsieur McCracken," Moustache replied. "You were commissioned by Monsieur Auzepy to undertake a mission, which I wish you to decline."

I shook my head, slowly and sadly. "I think I foresee a problem here," I explained. "You see, I gave my word, and I can't go back on it. That's what makes us different from those of you who work for the Kaiser."

Moustache's nose wrinkled and his lip curled. "You mistake, monsieur. I do not work for the Germans."

"Then who?" I blinked, taken aback for the moment.

"There is no need that I should answer that question, monsieur," said Moustache, "but I believe I have a solution to our little problem. If you are unwilling to inform Monsieur Auzepy that you cannot fulfill your mission, I shall make you *unable* to fulfill it." He raised the Luger, so that he held it at arm's length. "I had hoped you would be reasonable, monsieur, but I see that reason has long been absent among the English."

"I resent that statement!" I snarled, balling my fists. "I am a Scot, not an Englishman!"

"English, Scotch, you might be German. It makes no difference to me, monsieur.

"But to me," said Fritz, emerging from behind one of the ventilators, "it is a *very* great difference!" He reached out, seized Moustache by the wrist, and shook him. The Luger flew out of the Frenchman's grip and clattered across the oak planks of the deck. I lunged out, seized the pistol, and turned it on the Frenchman.

"*Sacré Bleu!*" cried Moustache.

"Thank you, Fritz," I said. "You have a gift for turning up at the right moment."

"A short break I have, Herr McCracken," answered Fritz, pinioning one of Moustache's arms behind his back, "from my duties in the galley."

"Well, I'm happy to see you making constructive use of it." I turned to Moustache, who struggled a little, vainly, in Fritz's grip. "Who are you working for?" I demanded.

"I shall tell you nothing," replied the Frenchman in surly defiance.

I glanced up at Fritz. It occurred to me that his remarkable appearance might work to our advantage. "I think Fritz here knows lots of ways to persuade you." To emphasize the point, Fritz snarled like a dog in his ear. "If you ask him nicely, he might show you a few."

"Do you think there is anything you can do to make me afraid, Englishman?" demanded Moustache, with a sneer. "When you meet the one I follow, you will wish you had done as I suggested."

Fritz said something in German, and shook him roughly. He seemed to wilt, cringing and looking fearfully over his shoulder at Fritz's wild red hair and his odd eyes. "Very well, very well!" he bleated. "I will tell you what you wish to know." I blinked in surprise. What a change of heart! "May I please have a cigarette?" he pleaded.

"Of course," I said. "Fritz, you can let him go."

Moustache slouched against the railing, and Fritz took the opportunity of drawing his Mauser and sliding off the safety. The Frenchman's eyes flicked from side to side. Then, as he drew a pack of cigarettes from his pocket, the sunlight caught something shiny between his fingers, something that wasn't a cigarette.

"Fritz, stop him!" I yelled. Fritz jumped forward, but already the Frenchman had thrust the shiny object between his teeth and bitten down hard upon it. He cried out and clawed at his heart, sinking towards the deck. Fritz caught him, and I tried to pry his mouth open, but to no avail.

"You Englishmen," he said, his teeth gritted and foam appearing between them, "you know nothing. You do not know who you face: the greatest man in the world, the strongest, the most to be feared. He hears from the spirits who ride the wind. He will know you are after him, he will find you, and he will kill you himself."

"Who will kill us?" I demanded. But it was too late. His eyes closed, and his head fell to the side. "God rest his soul," I said, crossing myself.

"He was of his master more afraid than of you, Herr McCracken," remarked Fritz, also crossing himself.

"But who is his master?" I wondered. "Who could be so terrifying he'd rather die than betray him?" After a short pause, I added, "You'd better fetch Captain Evans, and the ship's surgeon."

After a few minutes, Fritz returned with Captain Evans and another officer in tropical whites.

"Well, this is a rum do, McCracken, and no mistake." Captain Evans looked on as the doctor stooped beside the dead man. "What was he after, boyo?"

"He wanted me to refuse my assignment." I gave him a brief synopsis of where I'd seen him before. "It sounds as if someone doesn't want me to salvage the Corkindrill," I finished.

The ship's doctor looked up. "Cyanide," he said. "You know, the same stuff Gavrilo Princip tried to take."

"Oh yes," replied the captain. "I remember—the chap who assassinated the archduke and started this whole bloody war."

"Except that Princip didn't have enough cyanide to kill himself," the doctor went on, "and it just made him sick until he was caught. But this poor fellow had plenty. he's deader than Hippocrates."

We buried Moustache at sea that afternoon. The breeze was edged with cold, and as I listened to the beautiful words of the burial at sea, I reflected on how much more dangerous my mission had now become.

After ten days of uneventful sailing, I woke one morning to a respectful knocking at the cabin door. I threw on my dressing gown and inched the door open.

"Captain's compliments, sir," said an annoyingly chipper Benson, "but he asks if you wouldn't mind joining him on the bridge. We've made the rendez-vous with the *Despite*."

"Then we must be near the site of the sinking of the *Voltigeur*." Benson nodded at my observation. "Tell the Captain I'll be with him presently." I closed the door, then quickly dressed, kissed Ari and Archie, and followed Benson to the bridge.

With Evans was another officer, who had ginger hair and keen blue eyes. Three stripes edged his sleeve instead of four, indicating he was not a full captain.

"Sebastian Carter, Commander, *HMS Despite*." He had a good, solid handshake, decisive and honest.

"What's the situation, Carter?" I asked.

"I'd estimate the *Voltigeur* sank in about 500 to 600 feet of water—just in range for a John Brown."

"A what?" asked Evans.

59

"John Brown rig, sir," answered Carter. "Diving suit. Frankly, we're lucky she didn't sink a few miles to the west—the Calabar Canyon is far too deep for diving."

"Any enemy activity in the area, Commander?" Evans wanted to know.

"Nothing to speak of, sir," replied Carter. "Other than the torpedoing of the *Voltigeur*, nothing for about six months. As far as the war at sea goes, the Hun seems to have shifted his attention away from West Africa. There could be U-boats around, but we haven't seen any."

I looked out of the starboard windows at the sleek outline of Carter's torpedo boat. "Do we know anything about the *Voltigeur*'s location?"

"We've marked the most likely spot with a buoy. You can just see it there, sir." Carter pointed and, sure enough, there it was, hardly visible in the growing light. "We can't be certain, of course, but it's the best we can do, based on the reports of survivors."

"Thank you, Commander," I said. "We'd better get to work right away."

A couple of sailors had brought the John Brown to the stern of the *Amphitrite*, where it stood like a ghost in the grey light of dawn. The suit itself was made of rubber and twill, while the bulbous helmet was copper, with portholes to left, right, and front. Huge lead boots and a weighted belt finished off the panoply. Ari and Fritz had arrived ahead of me, and they were checking the rubber coils through which I'd be breathing during my dive. Some yards away, Assumpta held Archie, who was wriggling a bit. Assumpta sang him one of her lullabies, and he began to calm down. It was a wonderful gift that woman had!

Seeing my approach, Ari pointed to the breathing tube. "I've installed a wire in that and a small radio in the helmet, so we can talk while you're down there. It's an open channel, so you don't have to press anything."

"You're so clever, my love!"

"I'm not just a pretty face." That was true enough, though in fact her face was extremely pretty. She had been working on wireless underwater communication, a bit like the telegraph, in the years before the War, and we had used it on an earlier adventure in the Mediterranean. But here, the distance was just too great for that.

Suiting up for a dive is a lengthy process. First, I put on the rubber suit and strapped my feet into the weighted boots. Then I buckled on the belt, studded with lead slabs, and slotted my diver's knife and electric torch into place. Next, Ari and a seaman hefted the breastplate over my head and lowered it gently onto my shoulders, spinning the wingnuts until it sealed. Finally, they lowered the helmet over my head. For a few moments, I watched the three portholes spin past my eyes as they turned the helmet on its screw. By the time it was in place, the sun had brought a rich blue out of the pale grey of the early morning sky. Ari fetched Archie and held him up to me. "See Daddy in the funny suit?" she said. "Isn't he funny? Say, 'See you soon, Daddy! God bless!'" Stretching up, she kissed me through the open front port. "God be with you, love."

"And with you," I answered. Behind me, a pair of sailors had finished attaching my air hose. "I wish we had Jaubert's rebreathers," I lamented.

"I wish we had Jaubert." Ari closed the front port and tightened the lock. Instantly, the world fell silent, except for my breathing, which was deafening in the close confines of the helmet. Through the port, I watched Ari stride across the deck to the radio she had set up against one of the ventilators. A second later, static crackled in my ear, and a tinny rendition of Ari's voice said, "Mac, can you hear me?"

"Yes, I can!" I replied, jumping with fright. "You're very loud. Even louder than in real life."

"I'll turn it down a little, wise guy. Is this better?"

"Much." I stood up and, very ponderously, stumped over to the taffrail, where a ladder descended into the ocean. The buoy bobbed on the waves, about twenty yards away. One of the sailors took a steel cable and clipped it to a harness on my breastplate and belt. Two air-hoses and a steel cable: my lifeline. I gave the thumbs-up to the gathered crew, made the Sign of the Cross, and lowered myself down the ladder.

My feet were heavy in the leaden boots, and I had to concentrate to plant them on each rung. The water rose up my legs and then to my chest. When a high wave broke over my head, obscuring my vision for a moment, I decided that was enough and jumped into the cold embrace of the ocean.

At once, I felt the cable take my weight and slow my descent. I dropped through the glimmering submarine world, past a turtle that eyed me lazily and incuriously, through schools of silver fish that scattered as I neared and gathered together again above me.

When the phosphorescent hand of the depth-gauge on my wrist read about three hundred feet, the world began to grow dim. I turned on my electric torch and shone it down between my feet. I could see the muddy floor of the ocean, strewn with rocks, wisps of seaweed waving like the handkerchiefs of mournful women.

With a bump, my feet touched the bottom. The depth-gauge read 480 feet.

"I'm on the bottom," I told Ari.

A second or two elapsed, then Ari's voice crackled in my ear: "Do you see the *Voltigeur*?"

The odds had always been against my finding it on my first drop, but I looked around anyway. "I don't see anything like a ship," I reported, "but give me some extra cable, and I'll explore a little."

I tucked the torch into my belt so that it shone directly ahead of me. The ocean floor rose and fell like hilly country up above, but all was grey and dull.

Something moved, way above me, and off to my right. I turned to get a better view of it, wondering if it was some large sea creature, a whale or a shark, perhaps.

What I saw was a narrow shape, sharp like an axe-head. On its sides towards the front were what looked like stubby wings. It wasn't a creature at all, but something manmade.

"Ari," I said, "there's a submarine down here."

"A U-boat!" She sounded understandably surprised. "Where is it?"

"Above me, about a hundred feet. That's probably as deep as she can safely dive. She must be trying to avoid the *Amphitrite* and the *Despite*."

"Why would they do that? Why not just torpedo us?"

"She may be out of torpedoes," I suggested. "They don't carry more than about twenty."

By this time, I could see more of the U-boat's length. What I had thought of as stubby wings were actually the fins that controlled the submarine's depth. I saw that it would pass directly overhead. A horrible thought occurred to me, and I gazed back along the slack arc of my lifeline.

"Captain Evans would like to know the U-boat's heading," came Ari's voice.

"What?" Her words had stabbed through my concentration. The U-boat was close enough, now, that I could see its wake, like the tail of a comet. Ari was repeating her question, but I couldn't focus at all on what she was saying.

At that moment, the slender prow of the U-boat brushed my lifeline. A tremor ran down its length that I could feel echoing in my suit.

The lifeline slid down the side of the submarine until it reached the fin, where it lodged.

"Great Sc—!" I cried out. But the last syllable was cut short. The submarine passed overhead. I was jerked off my feet and flew through the murky water after it.

CHAPTER 5
SEARCHING FOR THE *VOLTIGEUR*

For a moment, I was confused and disoriented. The world spun around me, and I could feel the enormous pull of the U-boat's engines, all 3600 horsepower, keelhauling me through the undersea gloom.

Then I understood what had happened. The air hoses and cable were caught on the U-boat's fin, and it was dragging me along after it. I prayed fervently for deliverance, but quickly too.

It would not be long, I realized, before the submarine pulled me to the maximum length of the lifeline. Then the hoses would tauten and, even though they were made to withstand enormous strain, they would snap, and I would be stranded at the bottom of the sea, water filling my suit.

For a few seconds, I panicked. Of all the ways to die, drowning has always seemed the worst to me. I must have made some kind of panicky noise, because I heard Ari's tinny voice saying, "Mac, are you all right down there?"

The voice of my wife actually had a calming effect on me. "Ari, let me have as much length in my lifeline as possible."

"Why?"

"Please, just do it!" My temporary calm was over. My mind raced: I could estimate the speed of the submarine, and I knew the length of the lifeline. That gave me two minutes. What could I do in two minutes?

I craned my head back to look at the U-boat, ploughing through the waters ahead of me, its propellers churning the water into bubbles behind it.

There was nothing for it. I had to climb.

"Abut a hundred seconds," I said to myself, reaching over my head with one gloved hand to seize the steel cable.

"What?" said Ari. "Mac, what's happening?"

"Just an average day at the office, dear," I answered through gritted teeth as I pulled myself along the lifeline. The waters dragged along my body, pulling me back worse than gravity.

"Eighty," I said, under my breath.

It was like climbing a cliff during a tornado. Except that there was no cliff, and so no hand-holds. Just the rope. I reached up and seized the lifeline a little higher.

Suddenly, something struck my helmet with a terrific force, probably a rock. A noise like a church bell reverberated through the copper dome of my helmet, rattling my teeth. The force of it surprised me so that I let go of the lifeline, and my fingers trailed helplessly along it, clutching a few times at empty water. Panic rose in me.

"God, help me!" I cried out.

My fingers closed about the steel cable. I had caught it, but looking up I could see with something approaching despair that I had lost distance and therefore time as well. But there was nothing for it. I began hauling myself along it once more.

"Sixty," I said, though I was fairly sure that was only an approximation.

Hand over hand, I laboured up along the hoses towards the submarine. Behind me, the lifeline made huge loops of rubber and steel that waved back and forth in the currents as if they were alive. What if they were to get caught on something? I wondered.

"No," I said aloud, "enough of that. Forty." My arms were beginning to strain, and my fingers, in the thick gloves, were clumsy and frequently slipped.

"Twenty," I gasped as, with a sigh of relief, I saw the fin of the U-boat through one of my helmet's

69

ports. I reached out, took hold of it, and heaved myself bit by bit onto the top plane.

"Twenty," I grunted.

I curled my fingers around the leading edge of
the fin. The water buffeted my head and shoulders.
For a moment, all I could do was hang on. I could
see where the lifeline was caught, right at the joint
between the fin and the hull. I stretched out my
hand towards it.

Ten, I thought—but I didn't say anything. I
needed all my energy. Behind me, the lifeline con-
necting me to *HMS Amphitrite* had begun to rise, the
shallow curve stretching into a straight line. I had
only seconds left.

And the lifeline was stuck. No matter how I
pulled from one direction or the other, it was caught
in the fin.

"Lord, just free this for me," I prayed, "and I
promise . . . " I couldn't think of anything to promise. "Maybe we can talk about this later?" I wondered. "Amen."

At that moment, the Captain of the submarine
evidently decided to change the depth of his vessel,
because with a grinding noise that I felt rather than
heard the fin shuddered and shifted. As it did so, the
cable that had been stuck sprang out of the joint.

"Thank you, Lord," I said with a grunt, as I dragged the lifeline along the leading edge and free. Moments later I was floating away from the U-boat. I caught a fleeting glimpse of its propellers and its bubbly wake between my feet. Then it was gone, and I descended in slow cartwheels towards the seabed.

With a bump, I touched down. I bent my knees, dropped, and rolled, sending up a fountain of sand all around me. Then I was still and, to my amazement, alive. I lay there for a few moments, while my lifeline drifted towards the seabed.

"Mac! Mac! Are you all right?" Ari's voice sounded a little higher-pitched than usual, a sure sign she was worried. And I realized that she had been talking urgently all through my ordeal with the submarine. I had just been too focused to respond.

"I'm fine," I answered, pushing myself up from the seabed. My head was ponderous inside the copper helmet. I told her briefly what had happened.

"God be praised," she said. "Where's the U-boat?"

"Gone." I had managed to get myself upright, and was taking stock of my situation.

"Are your air hoses damaged at all?" asked Ari. "There's a nice young seaman up here who's very concerned about that."

71

"I don't think so," I replied. "But I think I'd like
. . . " My voice trailed off. I had been going to say
that I'd like to return to the surface, but now something new had caught my attention. It was hard to
be certain in the murk, but some yards away the seabed rose in a great swelling hill, and peeping over the
top of that was something that didn't look like rock
or seaweed. "I've just seen something," I told Ari.
"I'm going to investigate."

Unhooking the electric torch from my belt, I
flipped the switch, and instantly the yellow beam
picked out a hideous face with a massive underbite
and sharp teeth. I cried out in alarm.

"Mac, what is it?" demanded Ari.

Whatever the little monster was, it darted away
at top speed on seeing my light. I began to laugh. It
had seemed huge and terrifying, but it was less than
six inches in length. "Just a fish, Ari," I said. "It surprised me, that's all. An ugly wee beastie!"

I began my slow progress towards the hill. Each
footstep became ponderous as the ground rose beneath me. My breath rasped in my ears like an old
engine.

Above me, the shape I had seen slowly emerged
from the gloom, and I shone my torch along it, a
diagonal cut through the waters, like the line on

some murky graph. It was certainly the mast of a sunken vessel, I saw, my heart beating a little faster.

"It's a ship, all right," I told Ari.

"Is it the *Voltigeur*?"

"I can't tell yet." A few more laboursome steps, my knees and calves straining, brought me to the summit of the hill, gazing down on the wreck of a torpedo boat. With a smile of satisfaction, I reported to Ari, "Yes, it's the *Voltigeur*." Her deck and superstructure were exposed to me, as clear as blueprints. The bridge was directly under my feet, the funnel a little to my left. She had come to rest with her starboard side pressed against the side of the hill, which meant that the torpedo damage and the Corkindrill's egress hatch were both concealed. I would have to go inside.

A pale shape moved like a ghost through the beam of my torch, and my elation at having found the *Voltigeur* drained. I shone the torch back and forth, but could see nothing more. "Please, Lord," I prayed, thinking of a recent adventure in Mexico, "no more sharks!"

My descent of the further side of the hill was more cautious than my ascent had been. Should I slip, I might get stuck, or the suit might get damaged. The ground was treacherous, and more than once my foot scrabbled to find a piece of firm ground.

My torch picked out more and more details of the ship: the four-inch guns fore and aft, the torpedo tubes amidships, the helm, range-finder and binnacle on the bridge, the speaking tubes and the engine room telegraph with its brass handle still set to Half Speed Ahead.

In a few moments, my feet touched down on the bridge. The wreck had settled at a slight angle, so I stood with one knee bent and the other straight. With a little effort, I crossed the bridge to a ladder in the aft wall. As I reached out for the rail, a fish like a blue sausage with weak eyes and puckered lips hurried out of my torch-beam and into a speaking tube. It fit almost exactly. I swung myself down the ladder. The bridge, I saw, was almost literally a bridge: beneath it was an open space of deck, where ammunition boxes had been stowed against either wall.

I knew from the schematics that the Corkindrill's storage bay was amidships, so I made my way along the waist of the vessel, around the funnel and between the torpedo tubes.

The hatch leading to the hold was open already, and when I shone my torch through it, the first thing I saw was yellow eyes, staring back at me. But the fish scattered, and I saw planking and the steel ribs of the ship, between which boxes and tools had been strapped. But the space was empty.

"Ari," I said, "the Corkindrill's gone."

After a short pause, she said, "As we might have guessed."

"I'm going down into the hold. There might be some clues."

"Be careful," she warned.

"Am I ever anything else?" I wondered.

I tucked the torch into my belt and descended into the darkness of the cargo bay. When my feet touched the bottom, I flashed my torch around. One of the first things I saw was one of Jaubert's diving suit, with a rebreather, hanging on the wall. It was less bulky than a normal John Brown, with a slender helmet and tanks of compressed air. I told Ari.

"Just one?" she asked.

"Just one, and an empty hook. One suit and re-breather is missing." I turned slowly, flashing the yellow light from my torch around the cargo bay. "And the Corkindrill is certainly gone, and the bay doors are open." Looking through the doors, I aimed my torch aft. "Ari," I said, "I can see the tor-pedo damage." It was about ten yards away, a great gash in the side of the hull.

But something didn't quite add up about that damage, and I concentrated the beam of the electric torch upon it. I could see twisted metal and protruding struts caused by the blast, but there was something wrong about it all.

Then suddenly I realized what was awry, and gave a short gasp—although I should have seen it coming.

"What is it, Mac?" came Ari's thin metallic voice.

"I can see the damage to the hull," I said, "but the problem is, I don't think it was a torpedo at all. The explosion occurred inside the *Voltigeur*. It wasn't a U-boat strike. It was sabotage. The Cork-indrill has been stolen."

CHAPTER 6
ADVENTURE CANCELED

Back on board the *Amphitrite*, I stood in a puddle of seawater as Ari and a couple of seamen divested me, piece by piece, of the John Brown rig. I felt a bit like a medieval knight.

"Mr. McCracken," said Captain Evans, "I've taken the liberty of wiring the Inspector-General of the West African Field Force regarding your discovery down below." He paused in minor consternation. "Do you think you have a clue where it might have been taken?" He looked furtively left and right. "And by whom?" he concluded conspiratorially.

I shrugged. "By whom, I have no idea. Where? I'll need to see your charts."

Across the deck, Archie saw me, made a loud noise, and held his hands out towards me. Assumpta said something to him in Spanish and brought him over to me.

"See, here's your Papa," she said. He reached out and pulled my nose.

"I'll take him, Assumpta." Ari took the baby from her. "Do you think you could find us some tea?"

"On a British ship? I think I can manage it, *se-ñora*."

"She's a kind of a female Fritz, isn't she?" I mused, watching her depart. I stepped out of the suit and, moments later, we were on our way to the ship's operations room, where Captain Evans spread out a chart on the table for us. It's always interesting to see a nautical chart, covered with the little numbers that record the depth of the water. It's like the negative image of a regular map—all the detail is in the sea, and the land is largely blank.

I ran my forefinger along the coast. "The operational range of the Corkindrill is about four hundred miles. My guess is that the thief would take it as far from hostilities as possible, which would put it somewhere along the coast here, probably hidden in a lagoon. Do any of these territories still belong to the Germans?"

Evans shook his head. "They're all in our hands now, McCracken." He leaned closer to peer at the chart. "Well, there are plenty of lagoons along this coast. Some of them aren't even recorded on our charts. You'll need a native guide to find it, and it could still take weeks."

"We need a floatplane, an aeroplane that has floats instead of wheels, so you can land it on the water. The Admiralty has been developing one—the AD Type 1000."

"You think you can get one?"

"Else there's no point in being a Knight of the Bath. What?"

Ari, I saw, was smiling as she gently rocked Archie back and forth. "You," she said. "You're on an adventure again, and loving it." She kissed me on the nose. "It's what you were born for."

Before I could respond, a sailor entered with a salute and handed Evans a telegram. Evans dismissed him and looked up at me. "A signal from Douala, the capital of Cameroon. It looks as if we're in for a state visit from both the English and French representatives in the area." He folded the telegram in half and slipped it into his pocket. "Better comb your hair, McCracken."

It was more than an hour later that a launch came alongside and two distinguished-looking officers climbed the steps.

"Permission to come aboard, sir," said the gentleman in the lead, holding his salute until Evans responded, "Permission granted, General."

The steps clattered as he ascended them, a dapper man in his late forties, his uniform neatly pressed and a ribbon of brightly-coloured medals over his breast pocket.

"Welcome to West Africa." He thrust out a small, dry hand for me to shake. "Brigadier-General Charles Macpherson Dobell. Is this your first visit, McCracken?"

"I hunted a little in Kenya before the War," I replied.

"Well, you'll find this is a wholly different experience. Wonderful place, though, and full of wealth—copper, diamonds, aluminium, bauxite. You name it, this continent has it. Think of what we'd lose if the Africans could ever be persuaded to work together!"

The other officer, this one in the blue jacket and red trousers of the French Army, stepped out from behind Dobell. "That is why our aim as colonizers should be the eventual independence of the colonies, General."

Dobell's small eyebrows sprang up. "A remarkable opinion, General Aymerich."

"And unfortunately not one that my government shares. And in the end I am but a humble servant of the Republic of France." He shook hands with me. "It is my honour to meet you, Monsieur McCracken. I have heard the stories of several of your escapades.

I am Joseph Aymerich, General and Commissioner of the French Republic of Cameroon."

"I'm pleased to meet you, Commissioner." Evans ushered us along the deck towards the operations room. As we walked, Dobell said, "Well, we British are here for a number of different reasons, of course—partly to bring civilization to the savages, light to the dark continent, as it were. The profit motive is strictly minor."

"And to us also, *monsieur général*," said Aymerich with a smile, as we entered through the door Benson held open. "Africa is a rich continent, and easily exploited. But we, General Dobell, we are soldiers, not politicians. Our concerns are very different, *n'est-ce pas*?"

"Quite different, quite different," blustered Dobell.

We all took seats around a table on which was spread a chart of the Gulf of Guinea. Aymerich said, "Monsieur McCracken, could you please explain why you believe the *Voltigeur* was sabotaged?"

I took a deep breath, and as briefly as I could, explained my reasoning. When I had finished, I added, "I suspect Captain Strombourg—he and Jaubert are the only crewmembers who are currently missing."

81

Dobell gave an audible gasp, while Aymerich lowered his eyebrows a moment and stroked the little triangular beard he sported. "Do you know what you say, Monsieur McCracken? *Capitaine* Strombourg was a war hero."

"Given his war record, McCracken, it seems unlikely he'd be working for the Hun." Dobell paused reflectively. "Of course, the traitor might have been the diver."

"Jaubert?" I exploded. "Absolutely not! He has a war record too, General."

"But if it's not Strombourg, and it's not the diver, then who?" wondered Dobell reasonably.

"We'll know when we find the Corkindrill." I gestured towards the chart, and the two generals craned over it. "It's most likely somewhere along the Gold Coast—Togo or Ghana. When we find the Corkindrill, we'll find the traitor. I'll need a guide, a boat, and an AD 1000 floatplane."

"Oh, we'll take it from here." Dobell's eyes snapped up and locked on mine. "His Majesty's Government thanks you very much for your help, McCracken, and wishes you well in your future endeavours."

"Wait a moment. What do you mean?" My eyes became slits. "Are you saying I'm not to be included in this mission?"

"Well, yes, that's exactly what I'm saying." Dobell sat back in his chair and regarded me levelly. "Obviously, this is a job for military personnel, not civilian."

"But—I'm a knight!"

"So am I, McCracken—the same order as you, but the military division instead of the civilian." Dobell pressed his small lips into an infuriating smile. "I'm afraid being a knight isn't about going on quests any more. I'm awfully sorry. I confess, I hadn't imagined you would *want* to go on this expedition."

"Jaubert was my friend."

Dobell nodded. "I understand entirely, McCracken," he said, "but we can't allow personal feelings like that to interfere with the war effort. In military matters, I'm sure you'll understand, military personnel must be assigned appropriate duties, and you hold no rank in His Majesty's Armed Services."

"*Mon général.*" Aymerich turned to the British officer. "I urge you to make an exception in this case, given Monsieur McCracken's record and his friendship with the diver Jaubert."

"I'm afraid I have to put my foot down." Dobell shook his head sadly. "These matters are crucial to the Allied war effort, and must be handled by appropriate personnel." He rose from his seat and handed Evans a sealed envelope. "Captain Evans, your orders are to take Mr. and Mrs. McCracken to England." Turning to me, he added, "I believe a job awaits you at the Vickers-Armstrong Aircraft Company. Good luck, McCracken, and keep those bombs coming, so we can beat the Hun, all right?"

With an infuriatingly affable nod, Dobell turned on his heel and strode for the door. My fingers tightened on the arms of my chair. I wanted to punch him right on his small nose.

Aymerich rose, his sensitive eyes brimming with concern. "My sincerest regrets, monsieur," he said. "*Au revoir*. I hope we shall meet again soon." Saluting Evans, he followed Dobell.

Silence filled the operations room, till at last Evans stammered, "Oh, McCracken, I'm most awfully sorry." He stayed a moment, indecisive, then mumbling an apology followed the generals.

I made my way slowly from the operations room to my cabin, like one who has had his insides punched out. I've never sought adventures. They just sort of come to me. But to be denied one was almost more than I could endure, especially this one, this attempt to even things up for Jaubert.

I paused outside the cabin. The sound of women laughing came to me through the hatch. Pushing it open, I saw my wife and Assumpta, sitting on either side of the desk, which now bore a teapot and cups.

"Oh, Mac!" beamed Ari, "I don't know how she does it—Assumpta is such a jewel! Somehow, she found us some cookies to go with our tea."

"Biscuits, *señora*, biscuits," Assumpta corrected her.

"Of course." Ari made a wry face. "The English sailors call them biscuits—not to be confused with the ship's biscuits, which are riddled with weevils." She frowned. "Is something wrong?"

Assumpta rose on the instant. "*Iré la vez, señora*," she said, sweeping the tea things away and exiting with remarkable alacrity.

Ari rose and took my hands in hers. "What's wrong, Mac?"

I had to work my jaw to be able to speak at all. "I've been taken off the case. They don't want me." Ari searched my face for a while in silent concern. "This is a military matter, and I'm a civilian. But they'll take us to England, to Vickers-Armstrong."

Ari's beautiful eyes narrowed as she looked deeply into mine. "Didn't you want to give up adventuring and work for Vickers-Armstrong?"

"I wanted to give it up, not be kicked off it." I dropped onto the edge of the cot. "I feel like such an idiot. I wish I hadn't gone diving for them."

"That thought's unworthy of you." When I looked up at Ari, I saw that her jaw was set in that determined way she had about her whenever I was doing something wrong. "If diving for the Corkindrill was the right choice at all, it was right you did it. You were the best man for the job."

"I'm the best man for this job too. They won't be able to find the Corkindrill without me."

Ari sat beside me on the cot and smoothed a stray lock of hair from my forehead. "That doesn't mean you were wrong to accept the job in the first place. They're in the wrong, but that's their problem, not yours." A little noise a bit like a creaky door came from the corner of the cabin and she turned to pick up Archie from his crib. A few minutes after this, Fritz appeared to announce that dinner was served in the *Speiseraum*, by which he meant the wardroom.

The following morning, I was awakened by a gentle rap at the hatch, and I threw on my dressing-gown and opened it a crack.

"Captain's compliments, sir," said Benson, handing me an envelope, "and a telegram arrived for you."

Closing the door, I ripped open the envelope and pulled out the folded sheet of paper.

"What is it, Mac?" Ari had propped herself up on one elbow and stared drowsily at me from behind tousled hair.

I held the paper up to the light from the porthole and read the telegram aloud: "McCracken, HMS *Amphitrite*, urgent, stop. Please come at once to Old German Govt. HQ Douala, stop. Aymerich, stop."

"Enigmatic," observed Ari.

I screwed the telegram into a ball and pitched it into the waste basket. "It looks like the French want me to build bombs now."

An hour later, I stepped out of the *Amphitrite*'s launch and onto Douala's wharf. It had been the scene of bitter fighting a year and a half ago, and the warehouses and harbour offices were still shattered, their windows open to the sky, the tops of their walls ragged. The street was pock-marked with shell-holes.

"Mr. McCracken?" An African soldier in a light khaki uniform and a corporal's stripes snapped to attention before me with a smart salute. He wore a fez, and his uniform stopped just above the knees. He wore no shoes. "I am Corporal Eduzi. I have a car waitin', sir." He led me towards a parked Crossley 20/25. She was a lovely old lady, like all her sisters, but she had seen better days. Her body was dented here and there, and she was rusty in one patch. One of her rear mud-guards was broken. But the red leather upholstery inside still shone in the bright equatorial sun.

"Does she drive well?" I asked Corporal Eduzi as I climbed in.

"She?" Eduzi looked at me blankly for a moment. "Oh, the car—not bad, sir, not bad indeed. We have her on loan from the British, sir. She gets maybe fifty miles an hour in the right conditions. Douala's not the right conditions, though. Pardon me, Captain—cars are not usually my thing. More of a boat man, me, Captain. I guided many white men into the forest, sir, many crazy white men, before this rotten War." He closed the rear door, turned smartly and cranked the ignition. When the engine caught, he climbed behind the wheel and threw the car into gear.

88

The trip really rattled my bones. The Crossley's suspension was fine, but Eduzi swung the vehicle wildly between shell-holes without reducing his speed at all. It felt as if we were making the motor-car's full 50mph right here in town. I gripped the upper edge of the door, my knuckles whitening.

"Do you drive boats this way?" I asked, as the Crossley's passenger-side wheels left the road surface a moment and bumped down on the straight.

"Nah, not me, Captain," answered Eduzi. "Boats into the forest, they go a lot slower than cars. No shell-holes in the river, sir."

I grinned. "But you still swerve round crocodiles, don't you?"

"Sometimes, we cut it a bit too close, Captain." Eduzi held up his left arm. The sleeve, I saw with a gasp, was empty. How had I not noticed before that he'd lost a hand? Eduzi's eyes and mine clicked in the wing mirror. His face split in a wide grin and fingers jumped out of the empty sleeve. "Only kiddin'!" he guffawed.

I joined in the laughter, and sat back to enjoy the rest of the ride. Further away from the wharf, some of the buildings had been repaired, but most were still empty shells, streaked with black where fires had raged. Many of the pedestrians wore native robes of fantastically-patterned red, yellow, and black. Often, the women carried baskets on their heads. Some soldiers mixed with them, mostly natives in fezzes, but some Europeans too.

At length, we parked in front of a two-story building with a wide verandah. A sentry stepped forward and, saluting, opened my door and then the wrought-iron gate. "See you later, Eduzi," I said.

"You bet you, Captain," answered Eduzi, stepping on the accelerator and roaring away in a cloud of dust.

Aymerich awaited me on the verandah, reclining in a wicker chair with a carafe of a deep red drink and two glasses. "May I offer you a glass of *jus de bissap*?" He poured me a glass. "They sell it everywhere here—on the street, at the train station, at the markets, the bissap vendors are everywhere. How do you like it?"

"It tastes a little like cranberry juice," I observed, lowering myself into another wicker chair.

"Aymerich nodded. "But it is made from hibiscus petals. I prefer it with a little ginger. It gives it a certain *snap*, do you not think?"

I took another sip. "It certainly does."

For a few moments, we watched the passersby without saying anything. Then Aymerich said,

"Brigadier-General Dobell loves the rules, I think, but he is right about Africa—it is a rich continent, which the Europeans have sought to plunder for decades. The only excuse I can offer is that French rule is more genial than German. We do not amputate the limbs of our native workers for failing to meet their quotas."

I winced. "They do that?"

"*Did* that, monsieur, *did*." Aymerich took a long pull at his bissap. "If the Germans have the Corkindrill, I think they will be able to take Africa back from us, do you not think so also?"

I didn't dare say anything. I thought I had begun to see why Aymerich had summoned me.

"You do, of course," Aymerich went on, "and that is why you were disappointed that Brigadier-General Dobell wanted to assign someone else to this mission, *n'est-ce pas*? That, and the fact that your good friend Nicolas Jaubert was killed for the Corkindrill. This makes the mission—ahem—personal for you."

"But still I think I could treat the adventure calmly and dispassionately, General Aymerich. I want to help the Allies get the Corkindrill back—I don't want revenge for Jaubert."

"Of course, Monsieur McCracken. We are not savages. We do not wish for revenge."

"But I can't take the adventure," I protested. "I'm civilian, not military personnel."

Aymerich shrugged. "If you wish to remain a civilian, of course, you may do so." He reached into his pocket and drew out a pair of little golden stars. "But if, on the other hand, you would like to follow this adventure, I am authorized to offer you a the commission of lieutenant in the *Armée Française*. It is a temporary rank, and will last only until the Corkindrill is recovered or destroyed. Should you accept this commission, Monsieur McCracken—Lieutenant McCracken—you could begin assembling your team this afternoon." He raised his eyebrows. "Will you accept?"

And that's how I got to serve in the French Army during the Great War.

CHAPTER 7
JOURNEY INTO AFRICA

Aymerich was not able to get us a floatplane, just a wretched, mangled old steamboat. The engine looked like it has been built in the Industrial Revolution. Some of the pistons and one of the crankshafts were bent, and I was tapping one back into alignment, when a sudden shadow fell across the doorway. I grinned, for Eduzi stood there, framed by the bright African sunlight. He saluted.

"Reportin' for duty, Captain!" he beamed.

Standing, I wiped my hand on my trousers and shook his warmly. "It's good to see you, Eduzi. You said you were good with boats—that's why I asked for you."

Eduzi's eyes ran over the smelly, dirty engine room. "This ship, Captain," he said, "she don't need a sailor. She needs a priest." I laughed. "The Commissioner, sir, he says we're sailin' along the coast."

"North and west," I confirmed.

Eduzi thought about that for some moments. "Close by, those are my people," he said slowly, as if chewing carefully on each word before swallowing.

"But a little ways off, those are the Crocodile People. You don't want to trust them, no sir."

"What's wrong with them?" I wondered.

Eduzi narrowed his eyes. "Those fellows," he said, "they worship the Crocodile God. And I don't know how they do it, but sometimes, they say, they make themselves into crocodiles. They go into a little hut, full of steam and smoke, and they come out crocodiles. Eduzi doesn't believe in stuff like that, Captain. But them Crocodile People, they're bad news, you bet." Making the Sign of the Cross, he added, "Pray we don't have to go so far, Captain."

"We'll have to go far enough to find what we're looking for. We're searching for something."

Eduzi nodded as if suddenly the recipient of great wisdom. "We're all lookin' for somethin', sir. And sooner or later, we're goin' to find it, you bet."

Eduzi and I spent the rest of the day fixing the engine, and we set sail the following day, chugging along the coast, trailing an oily cloud from the tall funnels. The coast we sailed along seemed bland and featureless for the most part, as if we were steaming into the half-formed world just before God had finished creating it.

Ari joined me at the rail on the top deck, her face shining as it did at the beginning of an adventure.

To me, she never looked more beautiful that at those moments, and I felt my heart melting to see her with Archie nuzzling under her chin.

"I've never visited Africa before." She breathed the salty air in deeply. "It's so exciting." She kissed Archie on the darkening patch of soft hair atop the pink dome of his head, and waved a vague finger at the formless trees. "It's so dark green it's almost black. It's savage and mysterious and inviting, all at once. It reminds me of the fairy tales I read as a girl. You go into a forest to earn your fame and fortune. And think of all the people tucked away among those trees—people who have led the same kinds of lives since the beginning of history."

"The Crocodile People," I agreed.

"The who?"

"The Crocodile People," I repeated. "Eduzi told me about them—they worship a crocodile god. He doesn't sound like a very nice god."

"Most ancient gods aren't nice," Ari answered. She pointed as a bird swooped close to the boat. Its chest was russet, its head striped. "That's a plover. There's one of your Crocodile People. They're called Crocodile Birds around here because they help croc-odiles by picking their teeth."

"Not very intelligent birds," I observed.

We stopped frequently. Sometimes, we landed at a settlement to take on supplies, but more often, Eduzi spotted a lagoon, which we had to investigate. They all looked the same to me: palm trees and white sand, and no sign of the Corkindrill.

"It's like trying to find a needle in a haystack," I complained to Fritz.

Fritz frowned. "What does this mean, needle in haystack? What is a haystack?"

I opened and closed my mouth a number of times. "A haystack," I explained, "is a stack of hay. A pile of hay. A big pile. You know, hay."

"Hay? *Heu*? *Eine Heuhaufen*?" Fritz snorted with laughter. "Herr McCracken, why would I in one of those put my needle? It would be stupid."

"It's just an expression we have in English, Fritz. It means it's difficult to do."

Fritz shook his head in bemusement. "This English," he said. "It is no wonder so long it takes to learn it. It is very hard to learn."

"It's not half as hard as German," I replied, "with all those super-long words." I frowned. "Aren't you hot in that suit?" I asked. He wore a white uniform, like a butler's.

"*Nein*, Herr McCracken," replied Fritz. "Hot weather for shabby clothes is no excuse, I think."

96

The heat was oppressive, except when a breeze blew off the sea in the morning, and off the land in the evening. In Jamaica, they call them the Doctor's Breeze and the Undertaker's Breeze. Only Assumpta seemed unaffected by the heat, and she was tireless, hurrying to and fro with the baby, fetching things, helping Fritz in the galley.

But when, a few days later, a cool breeze blew across the deck from the sea in the mid afternoon, Eduzi narrowed his eyes into the south.

"I don't like that, you bet you, Captain."

"What's the problem?" I handed the helm to Fritz and joined our guide on the port-side.

Eduzi pointed to the tiniest smudge of darkness that discoloured the almost invisible point where sea and sky met. "We better find a safe place to land. This is a big one, you bet."

Within an hour, the wind had freshened, kicking up white-caps on top of the waves. The little boat rocked side to side. We had closed all the windows on the bridge, and rain rolled down them in big shining drops. The sky was like a sheet of iron, the sea like coarse stone, and they ground our little boat between them.

97

The door opened and, for a moment, a gale whirled around inside the little room. In a moment, Ari stood beside me.

"Shouldn't we land?" she asked. "The shore is close enough."

"God bless you, Mrs. Captain," said Eduzi. "The beach is no safe place. The storm will find us there, you bet. You trust Eduzi—he'll find you an inlet or a lagoon, somethin' like that. The sea's not really his thing, but he knows one or two tricks."

The boat lurched, and I found myself slammed against the starboard wall of the bridge house. Ari cried out. For a terrible moment, we could see grey sky through the port windows, grey sea through the starboard. The helm spun. Lightning sparks flashed as the iron sky met the spinning whetstone of the sea.

Then, for a moment, the wind relaxed, and slowly the boat righted itself. Eduzi jumped for the helm, and together he and I struggled with it until it stopped its crazy circles.

"Archie," said Ari. The deck was heaving, and she staggered as if half-asleep.

"Ari!" She turned in the doorway, bracing herself with one arm. I had been going to caution her against going out into the storm, but then I remembered Archie. "Be careful," I said, lamely.

"Pray for me," she said, and went out into the dark.

Fritz's voice came from the speaking tube: "Herr McCracken, can you please to come here at once? There is a problem with the engine, I think."

"I'll be right there, Fritz," I said. He had been shoveling coal in the engine room. It was only a one-man job, being such a small boat, but it sounded as if things were beginning to escalate. I rushed out into the night.

The waves were high now, dark walls towering over the top deck of the little ship. They broke against the deck as I staggered along the rail, clutching it for dear life. The wind rasped and filings of cold water lashed me. Lightning flickered across the sky, revealing a wide beach and fringe of trees off to my left. I could see Ari ahead of me, hauling open a door into the cabin where she had left Archie with Assumpta. I pulled myself along the railing and lurched down the steps into the engine room.

Fritz's strange eyes were wide with fear. "Herr McCracken, I see that the pressure in the boiler is low, so more coal I put on, but the pressure does not rise, and now for the boiler I am worried."

99

Behind me came a popping sound, and we both turned to see that a rivet had come loose and sea-water was spraying into the hold.

"Try and secure that, will you, Fritz?" He hurried towards the leak, while I looked at the pressure gauge. It did indeed seem like low pressure, yet the boiler was very hot—I could feel the heat from some distance. I tapped the glass on the gauge a couple of times, and to my dismay, the needle jolted as if waking up and moved from where it was into the red zone: danger.

"Great Scott!" I said under my breath.

The sound of Fritz hammering a new rivet into place came from behind me, but even as he finished, another popping sound came from a different part of the hold, and the sound of spraying water followed.

"Fritz, we're in a great deal of danger," I said. "We need to get out of here, now."

"But, Herr McCracken—the plates are coming loose. I must fix them."

I took him by the arm and led him firmly up the steps towards the deck. "It's too late, Fritz," I said, but could add nothing further because of the noise of the gale. With my face inches away from Fritz's, I yelled: "Get Mrs. McCracken and Archie and Assumpta out of their cabin and to the wheelhouse. Can you hear me?"

Fritz nodded, and threw himself through the door as I laboured my way back to the wheelhouse, where Eduzi was struggling with the helm.

"Hard a-starboard, Eduzi," I said. "We have to beach the ship."

"God bless you, Captain," replied Eduzi. "Sea not usually my thing, sir, but I know the beach will not protect us from the storm, and how—?"

"No time to argue, Eduzi." I took the wheel from him and turned it hard to the starboard. "That pressure gauge in the boiler room," I explained, "it got stuck, and Fritz built the pressure up until it was very dangerous. Now we have lots of little leaks in the hold. When the cold seawater touches the hot boiler, it will crack, and that will cause an explosion."

"I can fix the leaks," said Eduzi, moving for the door.

"No! There's too many, and they keep springing up in different places." The boat was beginning to respond to my turning of the helm. The prow bent towards the land, rising and falling as the waves passed under or over it.

The door opened, and Ari entered with Archie in her arms, followed by Assumpta and Fritz.

"What's happening?" she asked.

"No time to explain," I answered. "Hold onto something firm. I'm going to beach the boat."

Ahead of us, we could see the white strip of the beach and the dark forest, so dark that it seemed to drink the night and absorb its lightlessness.

"Here we go!" I cried.

"*Heilige Mutter Gottes, bete für uns!*" Fritz shouted above the noise of the storm.

Good idea, I thought, and made the Sign of the Cross.

At that moment, it seemed that some titanic force shuddered through the whole ship. Eduzi and I were tossed to the deck as the ship listed heavily to starboard. At the same time, the stern rolled around. The prow, snagged on a rock, was the pivot around which the entire vessel described a ragged circle until the stern too hit an obstruction and it rolled over onto its port side. Glass shattered, pieces of equipment, charts, tables and chairs flew through the air and cascaded all about us. Archie wailed in fear. Something hit me on the head. I felt it scraping against my skin, and the blood flowing, but I had no thought of it. I leaped to my feet as soon as the ship came to rest.

Then the boiler exploded.

For a few seconds, the sky was lit up with an orange light. The vessel shook, worse than she had when I had beached her. The shockwave hit us and drove the last fragments of glass out of the windows so that they tinkled furiously around us. Ari covered Archie to protect him. Bits of wreckage pattered to the ground or into the breakers all around us. Something heavy struck the roof of the wheelhouse, so that wood protruded downwards like stalactites. Then I saw something slide past the window: the mast had been knocked down by the blast. Slowly, the noise of the explosion and the shaking of the boat subsided, leaving us only with the chaos of the storm. I pulled myself up to stare out of the stern windows of the wheelhouse.

The explosion had ripped the whole aft third of the boat to pieces. One funnel had completely vanished, and the mast hung amid tangled rigging like a discarded marionette. I turned my eyes towards the shore.

"The forest will give us some shelter," I said. "Let's go." One by one, we all climbed down the side of the boat to the beach. I jumped down last of all, and we fought our way up the rain-lashed sand into the relative shelter of the forest. Over our heads, the treetops swayed back and forth, groaning as they did so. We threw ourselves upon the drenched ground or against the boles of the trees, too tired to care whether we were dry or not. Lightning illuminated the wreck of our ship.

"Ships of the sea not my thing, Captain," said Eduzi, "but I think there's no fixin' that one."

"I think you might be right there, Eduzi."

"I am sorry, Herr McCracken." Fritz's tone was agonized, his face a picture of bleakness in the flickering lightning. "This is my fault. I the boiler heated too much."

"And I failed to clean the pressure gauge," I answered. "If it had been reading accurately, you wouldn't have overheated the boiler. This is the kind of thing that happens—we have to take the adventure God sends us."

"But how will we the Corkindrill find now?" lamented Fritz.

"We'll have to discuss that tomorrow," I said; but my speech was beginning to slur; I was falling asleep.

Six pairs of eyes gleamed in the darkness, then five, then four. One by one, sleep overwhelmed us. Archie held out to the end, nursing away valiantly. But at length he too detached himself from my wife and slumbered while the storm rumbled and raged above us. At length, my eyelids grew heavy, and I slept.

I awoke once in the night. The storm had abated, and the moon shone through ragged clouds on the beach and the wreck. A figure was moving from the ship towards where we slept, and I stared at it, trying to discern if I knew it. I did: it was Assumpta, and she carried a bundle in her hand, no doubt of things she needed for the baby. What a jewel! I thought, to venture into the wreck on Archie's behalf. Somehow, I derived great comfort from knowing she was looking after him.

When I awoke again, it was in daylight. The sky was clear now. Eduzi had been awake before us, crouching on his haunches like a sprinter listening for the starting-gun. But Ari awoke, and Assumpta, and Fritz, and stared about them.

We were surrounded by the sharp points of spears, all of which converged on us. Fritz went for his Mauser, but fortunately thought better of it.

At the far end of the spears was a circle of fierce faces. Some of them wore fantastic headdresses, some of them had daubed their faces with white. One of them stepped forward. A little taller than the rest, his face was painted so that it appeared his mouth went all the way around his head, and was

105

filled with sharp teeth. He wore nothing but a yellow loincloth, and a headdress made of a reptile's skull. His skin was raised in scores of little lines that trooped like marching soldiers from his back, over his shoulders, and down his chest and arms.

"Who are they, Eduzi," asked Ari, clutching the baby tightly to her. "What do they want?"

"Who are they, Mrs. Captain?" repeated Eduzi. "They are the Crocodile People, you bet. I don't know what they want. Perhaps they want to eat us."

CHAPTER 8
THE CROCODILE PEOPLE

But if they wanted to eat us, the Crocodile People made no move at once. In fact, after a few seconds, I noticed that they weren't even looking at me. The focus of all the warriors seemed to be fixed on something a little past my left shoulder. I turned and looked.

"*Omo te oorun*," said the chieftain in an awed whisper.

They were all looking at Archie.

I stood, blocking the chieftain's access to my son. Behind me, Ari said quietly, "*Omo*. Eduzi, in your language, that means *child*, doesn't it?"

"Very similar, Mrs. Captain. Tongue of the Crocodile People, though, that's not usually my thing. I don't know what the other word means."

"He pointed up," said Ari. "Sky? Heaven? Sun?"

One of the warriors reached out towards Archie. I moved to interpose, but Ari called me off. "I don't think they mean any harm. If they did, they would have killed us by now."

107

The warrior touched Archie's foot, pressed his toes gently, then retracted his hand. Another warrior reached out and repeated the movement, then another, and another, until they had all made what looked like a simple act of affection.

The chief stepped forward. "*Jeka lo*," he said. And he repeated it, as if that would help us understand.

"I think, Captain," said Eduzi slowly, "he wants us to go with him."

The warriors picked up our possessions and led us along the beach, which was strewn with detritus from the storm, till at length we came to the mouth of a river. Here, drawn up out of the water, lay half a dozen hollowed-out log canoes.

"This is not helping us find the Corkindrill," I complained as we all climbed into the canoes.

"Patience, dear," replied Ari. "Remember, an inconvenience is just—"

"An adventure wrongly considered, I know." The canoe rocked as one of the warriors pushed us out into the stream. And then we were off, gliding down the shining brown stream. All day we plied our course, surrounded by the noise of birds and insects, but seeing none. Even in daylight, the jungle was impenetrably dark. At noon, the chief, who

108

rode in the canoe with me, offered me a mash made of yams and something peppery, which I ate hungrily. For most of the journey, I watched the chief's back. The bumps on his skin were actually scars, and they seemed to have been put there deliberately, for they formed geometric patterns. It must have been very painful, I reflected, to have each one of them cut into his skin, and I wondered what the purpose could possibly be.

After what seemed like an eternity, the river opened up into a wide lake. A large village stretched from the near shore almost to the margin of the forest. The thatched roofs looked like tousled heads, above which rose the clay walls of a large castle-like structure, complete with turrets and a large door in the front. Some men were standing in the shallows, bathing each other's backs. They paused in their ablutions and watched us silently as we paddled past them.

The canoes turned their noses towards the land, and in a moment, we had beached them and were stepping out. The chief of the people who had led us here leaped out of the canoe and shouted out to his people, who came crowding out of the village and onto the beach.

"Come and see the Children of the Sun." Ari was standing a little behind me, Archie asleep on her shoulder. She flashed me a grin. "I picked up a little of their language on the trip."

"Children of the Sun?" I was puzzled. "I thought these were the Crocodile People."

"I can't explain it yet."

The chief led us up the beach and between the huts of the village. Many of the huts were decorated with pictures of animals, very stylized, mostly crocodiles. The people crowded around us, their eyes wide, chattering animatedly to one another, pointing and calling to us. But they parted for us as we went.

"Eduzi," I said out of the side of my mouth, "why does he have all those scars?" I had been burning to ask the question all day.

"That's what I tell you about these people, Captain," answered Eduzi. "They turn themselves into crocodiles. Those scars, they make him look like a crocodile, and when he looks like a crocodile, he has the strength of the crocodile." He pointed back towards the lake shore. "Those men bathin' each other's backs, Captain, they just had the scars put on them. Bathin' helps soothe them, but it also helps raise those scars up big, like the bumps on the skin of the crocodile."

"How do you know so much about them?" I wondered.

Eduzi grinned. "Just guessin'," he said, "but you bet Eduzi's right about it, Captain, you bet."

At length, the chief stopped outside a large stockade in the shadow of the walls of the palace we had seen from the canoes. He led us through a courtyard and then into a hut. It was cool inside, and dark after the bright sun. But when our eyes had adjusted, we saw straw mats arranged in a circle about a hearth, on which a pot bubbled, giving off an aromatic cloud that reminded me how hungry I was by now.

A couple of women entered and spooned the contents of the pot onto plates, which they handed to us, while the chief indicated for us to sit on the straw mats.

"Aremo," he said, pounding his chest.

"What's he saying?" I asked Ari.

"I think he's introducing himself."

I stood up and pointed to myself. "McCracken," I said.

"Mackeren?" repeated Aremo.

"Close enough," I said, and introduced everyone else before sitting down to the meal.

Fritz's eyes had lit up. "Frau McCracken," he said excitedly, "this I can cook. It is crab, and tomatoes, and peanuts, and onions and cloves and other things—the ingredients I can get anywhere."

Ari spooned more of the delicious stew into her mouth. "It's certainly worth replicating, Fritz," she assured him.

Fritz finished his plate and took some more.

When at length we had eaten our fill, Aremo rose and pointed to me and Eduzi, and then the door. "Mackeren," he said, "*jeka lo.*"

"Captain," said Eduzi, "Crocodile People not usually my thing, but I think he wants us to go with him."

We rose from the straw mats, the women stepping forward to take our bowls with reverential bows.

"What's all this about?" I wondered.

"I guess you'll be finding out soon," suggested Ari, rising to kiss me in farewell. "Be brave."

"Most wives would say, 'Be careful,'" I pointed out.

"I know you won't be careful, so you have to be brave instead. But I know you'll be brave too. You always are."

112

"I love you," I said. "I can't imagine being on an adventure with anyone other than you. Let's carry on adventuring until we're old and have twenty children."

"I think we should." She kissed me again. "Be back soon."

Eduzi and I followed Aremo out into the bright African afternoon. The doors of the palace stood open, and he led us through them into a spacious courtyard. Flights of steps stretched from the sandy floor to an upper level. At the far end, in the shade, on what appeared to be a large wooden throne, sat a man who was the older copy of Aremo, and before whom Aremo bowed low. Grey hair poked out from under his crocodile headdress, and the bumps on his skin were large, as if he really had a reptile's skeleton. He held a knife in one hand and a stick in the other on which was the skull of a young crocodile. Ranged on either side of him were women of various ages, presumably his wives, and men, mostly older, who were clearly his advisors. What small bags we had rescued from the shipwreck had been opened, and the contents had been spread on the ground for the chief to see.

In the centre of it all was a golden statue, about eight inches in height, of a dancer with a feathered headdress, carrying a snake.

Kinich Ahau seemed oddly out of place in this new environment. The last time I'd seen him was in the office of the Governor of the British Honduras.

My mind raced. The package Assumpta had brought from the wreck—that must have been the golden statue. Assumpta, our nanny, was The Jewel, an international jewel thief! It was almost beyond belief. And how carefully she had executed her nefarious scheme, taking the job with us, knowing that we were leaving Central America at just the right moment for her own perfect getaway.

I thought of her holding Archie as I climbed over the side of *HMS Amphitrite*, of her somehow obtaining tea—*stealing* tea, no doubt—from the galley, of her playing with Archie, taking him for walks. I thought of how he would be quiet for her—for a thief!—when he wouldn't for me. Archie had been in danger of his life all that time.

And yet, something about Assumpta seemed honest, even though she was a thief.

I had to speak with her. And I had to speak with her alone. I had to convince her to confess, and especially to Ari. Ari trusted her implicitly. She would never believe me without Assumpta confirming my words.

The chief on the throne was speaking. I looked across at Eduzi, but my guide just shrugged and spread his hands. The words were incomprehensible to both of us. I looked at Aremo, and he pointed to the empty space between us and the throned chief.

A drum began to beat. It was joined by another, and then a voice. Then came beautiful, cheerful music, which reminded me of water bubbling merrily along a stream in the springtime. The instrument that made it looked like a xylophone with gourds hanging below it, presumably to improve its resonance. I learned later that it was called a *balafon*.

A small group of young men and women stepped out into the courtyard. They walked here and there, not quite randomly, greeting each other. One of the women slipped her arm through a man's. They looked very happy. Their dance became a little faster. They turned their backs to us and, when they turned back, the woman was holding a baby doll in her arms.

The dancers froze. The music ceased. After a moment, it resumed, but now the balafon gave out low, sinister notes, and the drum's rhythm was broken and irregular. From behind the throne emerged

116

one of the older dancers. He wore a huge head-piece that was shaped like a crocodile's head, and he swung a great tail back and forth. His scars were particularly large and impressive.

"Ombure!" cried the dancers.

"Ombure! *Ooni olorun!*" cried the audience in response.

Ombure thrust out his hand and crooked a finger at the girl who had just got married. She shook her head wildly and cringed away from him, but he moved in on her. He seemed to grow taller, looming over her. Her husband stood in front of her, but Ombure, with a single sweep of his hand, sent him cart-wheeling away. The same hand that had struck her husband now returned slowly for the girl. The fingers closed about hers. The drums grew faster, and Ombure danced, shaking the girl until she danced with him. Together they danced frantically around the perimeter of the courtyard, and then they were gone. All that was left was the abandoned husband, crying aloud over the baby doll in his arms. The other dancers tried to console him, but then began their dance again. The balafon's melody began again, slowly at first, but gaining in tempo and merriment. The dancers wove in and out of each other, sometimes acquiring a baby doll. All was happy once more.

Then Ombure returned. He danced through the happy villagers, his great tail swinging and sweeping. Out went the crooked finger towards one of the newlywed girls. The drums rose to a frenzy, the notes of the balafon staggered and lost their harmony.

Then all went quiet.

In the middle of the throng stood a man with a fantastic headdress, a knife in one hand, and a stick with a small crocodile skull in the other. He spread his arms wide, knelt on the ground before Ombure, pleaded with the crocodile god. But Ombure would not be swayed. Out went the finger and, with his shoulders drooping, the chief handed the newlywed woman over to him.

One of the young women, of a particularly remarkable beauty, stepped forward at this point and offered herself. The chief reacted with horror, holding his hands high over his head. He thrust the young lady aside and pointed at the one Ombure had chosen. The young lady, evidently the chief's daughter, went down on her knees before him, her hands clasped. But the chief ignored her pleas and sent the other woman off with the crocodile god.

Slowly, the chief's daughter rose, her face and shoulders resentful. She turned away from him and danced around the circle of villagers, once, twice, three times. The other dancers scattered, and there before her stood a tall man in white face-paint wearing yellow. It was as if he were on fire: yellow streamers wafted from his elbows, his hair was tied with orange and red ribbons, and golden ornaments were tied about his waist that flashed and rang as he moved. The drums grew softer, the balafon's notes slowed.

The chief's daughter passed a hand over her forehead and swooned, as if she were very hot. She tried to approach this newcomer, but fell back, swooning again.

He was the sun, and she could not approach him because of his heat.

The Sun reached up and removed his yellow headdress. He took off the yellow streamers at his elbows, and the skirt of gold. He became just a man. He took the chief's daughter in his arms and kissed her. For a while, they danced, advancing towards one another and then retreating. Each time they came together, they touched—hand to hand, eventually cheek to cheek. The Sun revealed an object he had concealed hitherto and handed it to her. She

119

parted the folds of the cloth that wrapped it about, and we saw that it was a baby doll.

A baby with a white face. A Child of the Sun.

The chief's daughter held the baby, rocked it back and forth, kissed it, danced with it. She whirled about, and the baby was gone. Instead, there was a young boy, white all over. Mother and son danced, until he was replaced by a young man, still white. The chief's daughter took him by the hand, and together they danced in a great circle, going in the opposite direction to when the chief's daughter had sought the sun-god. One by one, the dancers from earlier rejoined them, and eventually the chief. He was old, now, for the dancer had donned a grey wig, and he stooped and his legs were slow.

The chief's daughter brought her son forward, but the chief waved him away, his face wrathful. She presented him again, and once again the chief rejected his grandson. A third time and a third rejection. Woefully, the chief's daughter led her son away; but he went reluctantly, his body rigid, his lip curled with disdain.

And now the Child of the Sun went on a journey. Three times he danced in a wide circle, until before him stood his father, splendid in his yellow and gold. The Child went down on one knee before

120

his father, placed his hands over his heart, then spread them wide. The father pondered, trod slow and thoughtful steps around his son, his hand thoughtfully upon his chin. Then he reached into the folds of his golden garments and brought out a gourd, which he handed to his son.

The Child of the Sun held the gourd, danced around in a circle, and then went on another long journey. This time, dancers sprang in his way who were dressed like crocodiles. They wrestled with the Child of the Sun, but each time he threw them upon the ground and took up his journey once more.

At last, he came to a stop, and the music was silent. There, before the Child of the Sun, stood Ombure. The crocodile god advanced upon him, his hands held out to throttle the young man. But the Child of the Sun shook his head and held up the gourd. He raised it to his lips and sipped. The crocodile god, curious, took the gourd from him and sipped it. He seemed to increase in height, and his face lit up. He drained the gourd and danced. The music resumed, the balafon merry, the drums fast. Ombure danced and danced. He came close to us, so that we could see the shine of the sweat on his torso. It was a dance of exultation, of fierce merriment.

But then the crocodile god staggered. The music faltered, then resumed. Now it was slower, the notes deeper, and the balafon failed to keep time with the drums. Ombure reeled left and right. The liquor from the gourd was taking effect. Finally, he fell flat on his back and let out a loud snore.

The Child of the Sun tiptoed up to the sleeping crocodile god, drew out a long knife, and plunged it into his breast. Ombure woke up and stared into the eyes of his murderer. He scrambled to his feet and lunged for the Child of the Sun. But he was weak. He staggered, not through drunkenness this time, but because his strength was draining from him. He was dying. At last, he lay down, and now he did not snore.

The Child of the Sun reached out, and girl after girl emerged, dancing around him, wild with joy. They followed him in three large circles, until they reached home, where their husbands ran to meet them joyfully. Now the dance was more jubilant than it had been, until all the performers danced away and the music faded.

The sound of the jungle insects gradually emerged. I had been in a distant land and time for what seemed like many years, and now I had returned to the present. The sun beat down with its baking rays, and the heroes of myth stood no longer before me. They were dancers, panting with exertion, their bodies still at last.

I felt like clapping, but that would have been wholly inadequate.

The chief rose from his throne, and fixed his eyes upon us. "*Ombure ti pada*," he said gravely. Then, realizing we would not understand his tongue, he reached into his mind for other words. "*Ombure*," he said slowly, as if to dull children, "*laghachiri*."

Eduzi gasped. "Captain," he said, "the chieftain, he says Ombure has returned!"

CHAPTER 10
THE PATH OF OMBURE

What did they want?" asked Ari, when I returned from the palace. Archie sat on Assumpta's lap, and she was holding his hands and making him clap, so that he made happy purring sounds. I shivered. She held him with the very hands that had stolen Kinich Ahau, and God alone knew what else. "Well?" Ari persisted.

I shook myself, took a deep breath, and told them the story as we'd seen it enacted. "I think they think Archie is the Child of the Sun, and that he can somehow help them against this Ombure."

"Poor Archie." Ari took him from Assumpta and bounced him on her knee. "You have a lot to live up to, young man."

"But Herr McCracken," said Fritz, "why do they think this crocodile god has come back?"

I shrugged. "Some silly myth of theirs."

"They're not silly." Ari's eyebrows met over her perfect nose. "People put their most important ideas into mythology. In some ways, it's more real than history or science."

Now it was my turn to bristle. "Ari, that's absurd. How can superstitious nonsense like that be more real than science or history?"

Ari pointed through the window at the king's palace. "The man who was king a hundred years ago is dead now. His deeds have no effect on these people at all. But the sun still shines on them and crocodiles still terrorize them. When they tell the myth, they return to a time when they were strong enough to beat the crocodile. Living out their myth helps them in living out their lives. Science and history don't do that."

"Well, I don't think much of that." I put my hands on my hips. "How can sacrificing young women possibly help against crocodiles?"

Ari smiled. "Look at you, then, Mr. Scientist. You're getting all sentimental. It's a *very* effective way of dealing with a crocodile—if it's hungry, feed it. It's not nice, but it's effective."

Somebody gasped. We all turned to Assumpta. Tears welled in her eyes—crocodile tears, I thought. "*Señora!* Do you think they want to sacrifice Señorito Archie?"

I had not thought of that before. It was as if a cold hand had suddenly clutched my heart.

"If they hurt Señorito Archie," Assumpta insisted, and I suddenly realized that her tears were tears of anger, not of grief or helplessness, "they will do it over my dead body."

"I don't think they will," said Ari.

"Mrs. Captain," said Eduzi in a quiet voice, "these Crocodile People, they are a fierce people. Look at the scars on them. Hurt them; they don't care. And they will hurt you and not care. If they want to sacrifice young Mr. Captain, they will do it. What we have to do is get away from here, and as soon as we can. We need a plan."

"But I don't think they want to sacrifice Archie or anyone else," Ari repeated. "They're being very hospitable to us. If they want to make sacrifices out of us, it doesn't fit how they've behaved towards us."

"But we ought to take precautions, all the same," I said.

But we could not take any precautions right away, because at that moment, Aremo's wives returned with our evening meal. As we settled down for the night, Ari said to me, "I think I'm getting the hang of their language."

"You could understand their conversation at dinner?"

"I pieced together a little of it. It's a bit like Yoruba, which I was studying on the *Amphitrite*, and a bit like Igbo, Eduzi's language. They were talking about Aremo's half-brother. He was banished from the village for trying to kill the king, but he's hiding in the forest with an army of warriors. He's sworn to come back, kill Aremo, and become chief."

Archie gave a sigh, and pulled away from Ari. His eyes were closed, his lips parted, and his breaths came from between them almost without sound.

"I'm glad it was Aremo who found us, and not this brother," I said. "Sleep well, my love."

I dreamed that night of a crocodile who had a golden statue and a woman with long, dark hair, who tried to steal the statue. Just when she had it in her possession, a baby cried and she let the statue go.

Then I woke up, a little confused. The crying of the baby from my dream continued, and for a moment I wondered if I was still dreaming.

Then I realized Archie was crying. Aremo's wives were back, bringing more food with them. I said to one of the women, "Aremo?" She pointed towards the lake.

The sun had risen only a few degrees above the golden waters of the lake when I walked down the little mud street to the shore, where Aremo and his warriors were loading food and weapons into a flotilla of dugout canoes.

Seeing me, Aremo grinned. *"Jeka lo!"* he said, beckoning. *"Jeka lo,* Mackeren."

I joined him, and he indicated that I should help load the canoes up. I passed a bundle of spears to one of the warriors, who stood in the boat. "Where are we going?" I asked.

"Wha-ah we goin, Mackeren, wha-ah we goin?" Aremo parroted, with a grin, and continued stowing our supplies.

So much for that attempt at communication. I would have to wait for Ari to arrive. No doubt she would deploy the considerable gift she possessed for languages and not only find the answer to my question but have a complex discussion about philosophy in Aremo's language too.

It wasn't long before Ari turned up, and I framed my question to her. Turning to Aremo, she said, "Aremo, *nibo ni a ti lo?*"

Aremo pointed off along the lake, and talked for what seemed to me a very long time. When he had finished, Ari said something else in the Crocodile language, and to me added, "We're going three days' journey west, to a place called Ooni Ka Ona. I don't know what it means. I think *Ooni* means *crocodile* or *king*."

"Oh great, that sounds promising."

"You don't have to be sarcastic."

"We need to find the Corkindrill," I insisted.

"Whatever happened to taking the adventure that God sent?"

"Well, I just hope His adventure doesn't take too long, that's all. Is there any breakfast for us?"

Within an hour, we were boarding the canoes and setting off once again into the unknown. All day, we glided through the still waterways of that country until, when the sun was low, the canoes turned towards shore and we camped. Ari had spent the day learning their language, and she talked animatedly to the Crocodile Warriors. Assumpta held Archie about his pudgy tummy, talking into his ear now and then, no doubt explaining how he could best lead a life of crime. I saw my opportunity and edged closer to her.

"Assumpta," I began, "I wanted to have a talk with you."

"Yes, *señor*," she replied, and turned towards me. But then her eyes widened, and she pointed. I looked, and saw a shadow, about the size of a man, moving against the darker shadow of the forest. I sprang to my feet, yelling, "Aremo!" But the shadow was gone.

Soon after that, we ate our evening meal, and then we went to sleep without my having had a chance to talk with Assumpta. The following morning, as luck would have it, we rode in different canoes.

For two more days, we paddled on through the narrow rivers. Even Eduzi was beginning to lose track of where we were, and thought we might be in Dahomey or Togoland or the Gold Coast. We never saw the shadow in the forest again, though I noticed that Aremo kept a sharp eye out on the forest when we camped.

In the end, the river opened up into a wide mud-coloured lake. Peeking out from the tangle of forest were the remains of mud huts, like the ones in Aremo's village, but ruined, their roofs collapsed like the bombed houses in Douala. Aremo looked intently at the empty village, and I realized that the Crocodile People had once lived there. Why had they moved?

We plied on for another half-hour, then turned for the shore. When the prow of our canoe ground on the sand, Aremo leaped onto the beach, and I followed him.

"Mac," said Ari, joining me, "look at that."

Ahead of us, half hidden by creeping vines and thick moss, was the massive head of a stone crocodile, twice the height of a man.

"Ombure?" I wondered. Ari nodded.

Its eyes were slits of pure wickedness and corruption, its jaws gaped wide. And between them was darkness, unfathomable pitchy black. Archie looked up into the huge reptilian eyes and plunged his face into Ari's shoulder. He was really just tired, but he looked as if the monster had scared him out of his wits.

"*Ooni Ka Ona*," said Aremo, pointing at the crocodile head. "*Ri Ombure Ka Ona.*"

I took my torch out of my pocket, thumbed the switch, and shone the beam between the gaping jaws of the stone monster. The yellow circle fell on a path, slightly overgrown with ferns and moss, but clearly a road of some kind.

"*Ombure Ka Ona*," said Ari. "Of course: the Path of Ombure. I wonder where it leads?"

The Crocodile Warriors had gathered about us, and were all staring down into the darkness, feebly illumined by my electric torch. A few of them made plain by gestures that they wanted us to follow the path. Aremo said something that seemed to take a

131

long time to develop. Ari asked a few questions, and then reported her findings to me.

"They want us to take the Child of the Sun—they mean Archie—down the Path of Ombure, and destroy the crocodile god, who has been taking their people."

"What do you think, Captain?" asked Eduzi.

"If we do it, perhaps they'll help us find the Corkindrill," I suggested. "It's worth a try, anyway."

But before we could begin, a strident cry came from behind us.

"Aremo!" cried the voice. "*Jii dide—a je akoko lati ku!*" Out from behind a tree, twenty yards away, stepped a man who looked a lot like Aremo. His brother, I concluded, and probably the shadow I had seen in the forest, following us. He was tall and long-limbed, and his crocodile scars rippled as he moved. He held a bow in one hand, and an arrow in the other. Behind him emerged twenty other men, all armed with spears or bows.

"What did he say?" I asked.

"I think he said we're going to die," Ari replied.

Aremo's brother gave an order, and his warriors closed in for the kill.

CHAPTER 11
THE SASSYWOOD MAN

But the attack did not come. At the sound of another voice, the warriors paused and looked over their shoulders, nervous. Someone else had ordered them to be still. For a moment, I couldn't see this new commanding presence. Then a figure came out from the shadows of the jungle, short of stature, wiry of frame, and white of face. With a shock, I realized that I knew this person.

"Jaubert!" I cried aloud, and Ari gasped as she recognized him too. "They told me you were dead!"

"As you can see, *mon ami*," answered my friend, "the report of my death is—how is it Monsieur Twain puts it?—an exaggeration."

"Nicolas, I could hug you!" cried Ari.

"That would prove most difficult at the moment, *madame*," said Jaubert, "but *sûrement*, in a short time I would be happy to oblige. In the meantime, I must persuade Kekere here not to kill his brother."

For a few moments, Jaubert and Aremo's brother conversed, Aremo occasionally joining in. At last, Kekere thrust his chin out boldly and snapped, "*Iwadi Gomati!*"

133

"I don't get it," said Ari, shaking her head. "Trial by Gomati? What is Gomati?"

"It's a type of tree, Mrs. Captain," explained Eduzi. "Some people call it Sassywood. Trial by Sassywood is a way these people find right and wrong. Sometimes, they crush the bark of Sassywood into water and make the person who did the crime drink it. That Sassywood, it makes a man mighty sick, you bet you. Maybe even he dies. But if he confesses, the Sassywood Man, he don't make him drink it."

"The Sassywood Man?"

But before he could answer, Jaubert hurried over to us. "Now, *madame*, at last I shall do as you asked." He folded Ari in an embrace, and then me. "Ah, and the *petit* McCracken, *n'est-ce pas*?" He tickled Archie under the chin, nodded to Assumpta and Fritz, and shook Eduzi by the hand.

"Jaubert," I said, "what's been happening the last few months?"

"No time for the story now, McCracken," answered Jaubert. "I have persuaded these brothers to settle their differences by legal means, rather than by fighting. Both claim the right to be chief of their tribe."

"Have you been tracking us all this time?"

"*Oui.* That is, Kekere has been tracking you. When he told me of the *enfants du soleil* who accompanied his brother, I surmised it must be you." He grinned. "I knew you and no other would come to find me, *mon ami.*"

At this point, Aremo called out loud, and another figure joined us. This was an unassuming man, of shorter than average height and greying hair. He wore around his waist what looked like a mechanic's belt, but made from tree vines. In it were tucked various instruments—I saw the blade of a machete hanging from it, a small cauldron, a tripod, and a number of drawstring pouches. He carried a large canvas bag over his shoulder, and I could see that sticks and bits of wood protruded from the top of it.

"Watch, Captain!" said Eduzi. "This is the Sassywood Man. He'll sort these brothers out, you bet."

"Why don't they just take their concerns to a court?" I asked. "After all, wherever we are, it's either a British or a French colony. They can get justice from the Governor."

Eduzi smiled broadly, showing all his bright teeth. "But the Governor, he don't want to hear about stolen chickens or nothin' like that, Captain. And the courts are for *kwee* people—you know, rich men, with fine clothes and big houses. The white

135

judges, they will never hear the cases of the people from the bush and the forest."

At the sight of the Sassywood Man, all the Crocodile Warriors backed away and left him with Aremo in a wide and empty space of flat sand. A quiet fell upon that place, like shutting the bonnet on a humming motor. They didn't bow or salute or offer him any of the marks of respect they would accord to royalty. But they were respectfully silent and attentive.

Aremo took a gourd from his belt and offered it to the Sassywood Man. The Sassywood Man took it and raised it to his lips, drinking a long draught of water. I saw that beads of sweat had gathered on his brow, and his feet were covered with dust. He had made a long journey, and a thirst as dry as sand was upon him.

At last, the Sassywood Man lowered the gourd. He wiped his lips with the back of his hand, and for a moment he and Aremo regarded one another with understanding. The Sassywood Man nodded, and turned to Kekere. The same kind of unspoken conversation passed between the two of them, though Kekere looked resentful and just a little afraid. Then the Sassywood Man turned away and built a fire from the sticks in his canvas bag. He unfolded the tripod and hung his cauldron from it, pouring water into it. Taking one of his pouches, he drew out some pieces of bark, which he crumbled into the water.

"That's the sassywood, Captain," said Eduzi, nudging me.

The Sassywood Man laid out beside the fire the tools he would use in his bizarre lawsuit: a machete, some nuts that looked like coffee beans, and a flask of some oily material. Eduzi informed me these were kola nuts and palm oil. As the fire began to crackle and leap, the Sassywood Man began muttering under his breath. He picked up one of the kola nuts, placed it in his mouth, and chewed on it, muttering and chewing, and chewing and muttering. Occasionally, he paused to spit on the ground until a brown crescent shape formed about the fire. As he moved, he scraped a whetstone almost lovingly along the blade of the machete. The rasping was soft, and it mingled with the sound of the water lapping against the shore of the lake and the muttering of the Sassywood Man like a strange and otherworldly music.

"What's he saying?" I asked under my breath.

"It's a story," Ari answered me. "He's speaking to someone called Sagbata, who rules the universe. Long ago, Sagbata quarreled with his brother, Sogbo, who left the heavens and came down to rule the earth. Sogbo took with him all the wealth of their mother, Mawu, but he left fire and water behind because he was afraid they would burn and drown all his wealth. But when he got to the earth, he found his people needed fire and water to live, and so he sent the bird Wututu to make peace with his brother." She paused, while she listened a few moments to the Sassywood Man's chant, then went on: "Water and fire are very powerful. Who controls them controls the world. So Sagbata controlled Sogbo, but nevertheless agreed to send nourishing rains down to the earth. Before Wututu had returned, lightning flashed from the heavens, and the rains poured."

The Sassywood Man had finished telling his story and making his crescent, and now he turned back to the fire. It had burned down to embers. He dipped a sponge into the boiling water in the cauldron and wiped the blade of the machete down each side. He did this with an almost caressing movement, back and forth many times, muttering constantly. I heard the name Sagbata mingled in with the other words, but never Sogbo. At the end, he whirled round to the fire and plunged the machete into it. Stooping, he blew on the coals, which burst into fierce gold. Sparks jumped into the bright afternoon air. The blade began to glow. Turning to the onlookers, the Sassywood Man took another draught of water and spoke at length.

"He's telling us how all this is going to work," Ari related in a low voice. "He's here to find out who will be the next chief of the Crocodile People. Aremo and Kekere both say it's them. The Sassywood will catch the person who is wrong. He says it's best to say now who's wrong, to save the shame of the Sassywood. He'll give them each a kola nut to chew, and clean his leg with water and palm oil, then bring the machete close. 'If you are the true chief,' he says, 'the machete will feel cool as water; if you lie, it will burn you before it ever reaches you. So before the small shame turns to a big shame, just say, "I'm in the wrong." I'll give you till the machete is hot.'"

No one spoke on the little beach. Birds in the forest sang and squawked, and the waves lapped against the sand. The Sassywood Man placed a few more sticks on the furnace and blew on it some more.

When the time was up, the Sassywood Man turned to us and spoke again. "This is to show there's no trickery," Ari translated. The Sassywood Man took up the gourd and cleaned both his legs. He rubbed palm oil into them. Then he took the hot machete from the fire. The trees behind it wobbled in the heat haze. With measured strokes, he slid the burning blade up and down each leg in turn. To my amazement they were totally unmarked. The Sassywood Man returned the machete to the fire and beckoned to Aremo.

Aremo stepped into the crescent and stood next to the fire. In a loud voice, he declared his innocence and thrust forward his leg. The Sassywood Man cleaned it meticulously and rubbed palm oil into it. Then he drew the machete once again from the fire. He offered a piece of kola nut to Aremo, who took it and chewed on it fiercely.

"The kola nut," said Eduzi quietly, "they say it clears a man's head, makes it easier for him to hear what the spirits say."

The Sassywood Man swung the blazing machete through the air and touched it to Aremo's leg. The blade passed up his shin and down again. Aremo watched it with curiosity, but did not flinch; and when the blade was back among the embers, he grinned from ear to ear and riveted his eyes upon his brother. Then he strutted from the crescent and back among his people.

Now it was Kekere's turn, and he strode into the crescent, crushing the kola nut between his teeth and glaring at his brother as the Sassywood Man cleaned his leg and rubbed it with palm oil. The Sassywood Man took the machete from the fire and advanced upon him, the glowing blade held forward. Before reaching him, though, he gave Kekere one last chance.

"He just asked if he wants to renounce his claim," Ari explained. "He says, 'Your brother passed the Trial by Gomati. Better little shame now than big shame in a while.'"

"What did Kekere say?"

"What do you think?"

"Hm," remarked Eduzi, "this Kekere, he sure has a big monkey on his back, you bet."

Kekere, like his brother, had submitted to the crocodile scars; he knew pain. Perhaps he could endure the agony of the machete blade.

The Sassywood Man dropped down on his knees and brought the machete close to Kekere's leg. Kekere jumped like a spark from a bad electrical circuit, and the Sassywood Man paused. He looked up and asked a question, but Kekere said nothing.

The machete hissed. I saw smoke rise from the blade. Kekere cried out and leaped backwards. The Sassywood Man turned to us, the machete high over his head. He spoke in a strident voice.

141

"Aremo will be chief," announced Jaubert. "The Gomati has spoken." With a grin, he added, "See, McCracken? He is a very good lawyer, *n'est-ce pas?*"

Aremo was speaking to Kekere, who lay on the ground, his hands fastened about his leg. I couldn't understand the words, but he kept pointing at the forest and his meaning was unmistakable: banishment. Two of the Warriors came forward, seized him by one arm each and marched him to the edge of the forest. With a sullen glance backwards, Kekere limped into the forest until the shadows swallowed him up. No one followed him. Even the men he had led had abandoned him.

"What will happen to him now?" wondered Ari.

"He has been shamed, Mrs. Captain," said Eduzi. "Big shame. Now he cannot come back to his people. He must stay in the jungle because of his big shame."

"Can he ever return?"

"It would take a big deed to wipe out such a big shame," Eduzi replied.

And now the succession had been decided, Aremo turned to us.

Aremo spoke to us for several minutes, while Ari listened and occasionally asked questions. When he had finished, Ari informed us, "Aremo says that at the other end of this passage is Ombure. He wants the Children of the Sun—that's us—to trick him and kill him."

"If we do this, will he help us find the Corkindrill?" I asked.

"I asked him that; he says he doesn't know where it is, but he's willing to help."

"I don't know how to kill a crocodile god."

Ari grinned. "We'll find out."

"What provisions do we have?"

Fritz, who had been helping the Crocodile Warriors to unload supplies from their canoes, answered me. "We have nothing but yams," he said. "Yams, beans, and onions, and a few things I was able from the ship to rescue."

"Like what?"

Fritz turned out his pockets. "Just a little salt, and some garlic and cumin that in Douala I purchased, and two chili peppers. Ach, and this."

Reaching deep into his pocket, he brought out a small packet of rice. "And some thyme that to me was given by the cook on the Navy ship."

"Fritz, you're a one-man High Street."

"*Nein*, Herr McCracken, I have only the basics. But I will do what I can." As he turned to organize what food we had, he added: "And some chicken. The Crocodile People, they have a little chicken."

"We'll have to make do, Fritz. Well done."

"*Dankeschön*, Herr McCracken," said Fritz, stumping off to start a fire.

"We have no weapons," said Ari, "except what I have on me."

"Well, that should be enough to blow up a small country," I said.

"Just a couple of knives, my derringer, two small sticks of TNT, and a flask of tear gas." She thought for a moment, then added, "And, of course, the garrote. It came with the set. I don't like it."

"Nevertheless, it might be useful. I've heard garrotes are good for killing crocodile gods."

I looked at Assumpta, who was playing Peekaboo with Archie. The baby was giggling every time he found her. I still needed to find a moment to talk with her.

144

"Your son, McCracken, he is a fine young man." Jaubert had joined me. "His name is Archibald?"

"Archimedes," I corrected him.

"*Ah, très bien!* Archimedes McCracken." Jaubert tested the name out on his tongue, as if sampling a wine. "It is a good name. It is the name of a true adventurer."

"I had been hoping to give up adventuring," I said in a faint voice. "It's a wee bit dangerous for sproggins."

"Truly?" Jaubert gave a rich laugh. And just when it seemed to be subsiding, the laugh began again spontaneously, rocking his frame and forcing him to sit upon a fallen log while he wiped an eye. "That would be like a shark giving up his teeth, or the ocean giving up its salt." He gave another laugh. "Truly, McCracken, be serious."

"I thought I *was* being serious," I said. "It seemed like the sort of thing a good father does for his son."

Now Jaubert's laugh drained away, and he looked most sober. With utmost gravity, he said, "But what better thing could a father do for his son than teach him to be brave and to trust God?"

A wonderful aroma drifted past us, and I realized at once that Fritz had begun weaving his magic on the scanty ingredients he had gleaned. We all gathered around his fire, and he handed each of us half a coconut shell, spooning a dollop of golden stew into each.

"Soup without bread, Fritz?" I asked skeptically.

"*Ja*, it is regrettable, Herr McCracken," he replied, "but I think the soup you will find hearty and filling anyway."

We prayed Grace, and Jaubert raised the coconut to his lips. "*Ma foi!*" he declared. "It is a fine thing to be adventuring with you again, Fritz!"

It was a wonderfully spicy soup with yams, chicken and rice, that tingled as it went down. There was a hint of curry about it, and peppers to make it lively, and it was as he had assured us, extremely hearty. "If I ate this in an Edinburgh restaurant," I told him, "I'd be impressed."

"It is not difficult in an Edinburgh restaurant to be impressed by mediocre food, Herr McCracken," replied Fritz with a mischievous grin.

I laughed. "This is more like it!" I exclaimed. "This is what adventuring is really like. A little bit of minor discomfort, a little bit of danger, a lot of good food, and heaps of good company."

"And now," said Ari, "Nicolas, tell us your story."

"*Mais oui.*" Jaubert wiped the corners of his mouth with his handkerchief, cleared his throat, and began his story.

"When I heard the explosion aboard the *Voltigeur*, I was most curious. It did not sound the way a torpedo strike normally sounds. It sounded as if it came from within the ship. Naturally, I suspected foul play, and hurried at once to the cargo bay where we kept the Corkindrill. There, I saw that the doors were beginning to open, and to my amazement, Capitaine Strombourg was climbing into the Corkindrill."

"So Strombourg stole the Corkindrill!" I nodded. "I knew it."

"And yet, I was surprised," Jaubert said. "He has an impeccable war record—or had. That, at least, is about to change."

"What did you do, Nicolas?" prompted Ari.

"My first thought was to leap upon the Corkindrill, gain access to it, and fight Strombourg hand-to-hand."

"An excellent plan," I observed.

"*Oui, vraiment.* But, alas, not very practical. The Corkindrill locks from the inside. But nearby hung the diving suits and rebreathers we had been using in our trials with the Corkindrill. I quickly put

147

one of them on—the water was beginning to rise all around me, and I had to move quickly. Meanwhile, the cargo doors had opened, and I heard the release of the clamps that held the Corkindrill to the deck. I knew I had to act at once. I waded through the water and took hold of the stern antenna. Moments later, the Corkindrill's propeller spun, and the Corkindrill moved out through the bay doors and into the ocean, with me hanging on by the antenna."

I was amazed. "How long did you hang onto the Corkindrill like that?"

"It was about a day—five hundred miles. The Corkindrill, she is a very fast lady in water, if a little slow on land. Even now, I do not know what country we are in."

"We are in the Ashanti Kingdom," Eduzi told him. "This I figured out, while we were paddlin' along in them canoes. We were shipwrecked in Dahomey, and the Crocodile People, they took us through Togoland and into Ashanti—what you people call the Gold Coast."

"My greatest fear," Jaubert went on, "was that Strombourg would see me. Indeed, at one point, he stopped the craft and strode about on the deck, inspecting the condition of the Corkindrill. I was able to evade his gaze by slipping into the water and submerging myself or slipping to the other side of the vessel. When I heard the hatch close again, I scrambled back on board and took hold of the antenna. Moments later, the screw turned again and we were underway."

"How thrilling!" breathed Ari. Archie gave a little coo in agreement, and returned to his evening meal.

"Of course, I had no idea how long our voyage would be," Jaubert continued. "And, as long as I clung to the stern of the submarine, I could not sleep. By the time I saw land ahead of us, my arms ached with the effort of holding on, my head swam with weariness, and my belly growled with hunger. Furthermore, the air in my suit was beginning to smell very foul—I have never worn my diving suit so long in my life.

"The coast ahead of us grew and grew, and I saw a wide beach and palm trees. Beyond the palm trees, I could see nothing. The moment I felt the Corkindrill touch the sand, and heard the wheels begin to move, I leaped from where I had been hanging on. I found myself in about three feet of water, which concealed me perfectly. I raised my helmet above the water and watched the Corkindrill rise out of the sea and climb up on the beach. It headed directly for the palm trees. As soon as it was out of sight, I rose and waded ashore, removing my helmet as I did so. Ah, what a relief it was to breathe fresh air once more! But when I reached the palm trees, I found that the Corkindrill had vanished."

"Vanished?"

"*Oui—disparu.* Missing. Dropped from sight." He paused a moment, and the gentle sound of the waves filled the silence. "Beyond the palm trees was a wide lagoon—so wide I could not see the far side. The Corkindrill's tracks led into the water, but where she had gone upon entering the lagoon I could not discover. I was of course resolved to search, but the sun was setting and I was weary and hungry, so I knew I must first sleep and then search in the morning. And that is exactly what I did—using my diving suit, I began to explore the lagoon for traces of the Corkindrill."

"Did you find anything?" I asked breathlessly.

"Ah, *oui!* On the far side of the lagoon, I found a dam, cunningly camouflaged with vines and rocks. It had a sluice gate in it, and beyond it was another lagoon."

"And was the Corkindrill there?"

But Jaubert shrugged. "I do not know. Emerging from the water, I was surrounded by the Croco-

150

dile People, who were amazed at my diving suit. They seemed to think I was some sort of crocodile god, because I had been under the lagoon water so long. I stayed with them for several months, at first as a prisoner—a Child of the Sun, they said—but later as a friend and helper. It was my plan to return to Cameroon, to let General Aymerich know what had happened to the Corkindrill, but before I could do that, you came along."

Our attention was diverted at this juncture by Aremo. He stood and handed his coconut-bowl very courteously back to Fritz. Then he held out his hand and gave a command. One of his men handed him a lit torch. With the other hand, Aremo pointed towards the dark jaws of the crocodile god. "*Jeka lo*, Mackeren," he said, "*jeka lo*."

The eyes of all the Crocodile Warriors were on me. Ari, holding Archie, stepped closer to me and squeezed my hand.

"It's an adventure," I said, "not an inconvenience."

I held out my hand and Aremo passed me his torch. "*E dupe*, Mackeren," he said. Then, as if trying something new, he added, "Than' you."

"You're welcome, Aremo," I said, holding the torch over my head and plunging into the darkness.

CHAPTER 13

THE TREE OF FORGETTING

There's not really much to be said about a journey through dark passageways. It was cold down there, and noises came at us out of the darkness—sighing noises like horrible creatures breathing, or squeaking noises like giant bats, or creaking noises like loose floorboards. And it was a long journey, so that way before it was over I felt as if I'd forgotten what it was to have the sun shine on my face. And the darkness seemed to suppress our spirits. I wanted to talk to Assumpta, but I did not feel conversation was possible.

In all honesty, I have no idea how long it took us to traverse the Path of Ombure, but when at last we began to climb some more steps, and when I pushed aside some vegetation and felt the warm, humid air of Africa, we stepped out into the velvet night of the tropics, with stars shimmering down on us from above and a half-moon hanging above the trees.

Our first response on emerging from the underground path was to draw the sweet air into our lungs and just breathe with joy. We noticed nothing but that. But after a few moments, we became aware of other things. We were surrounded by trees, but to our left, the half-moon shone on a wide expanse of water—a lagoon, such as we had seen so many times on our search for the Corkindrill.

Ahead of us, about a mile, stood a hill, its crest silhouetted against the night sky and, now that we had begun to be aware of things, fringed with an orange light—a huge fire or many torches on the other side. The faint throbbing of drums came to us on the night air.

"Ombure!" It was Aremo who had spoken, and he shook his spear in the direction of the orange glow.

"Well, let's get going, shall we," I said, squaring my shoulders and getting ready for the short trek. We skirted the edge of the lagoon, the Undertaker's Breeze blowing cool against our faces. Every now and then there came from the lagoon the plop of a fish breaking the surface to snap up an insect.

"McCracken." Jaubert had hurried up to walk beside me. He seemed very excited. "McCracken, I might be mistaken—the time of day and my location are both very different, but I think this is the lagoon I saw weeks ago. Remember, the one protected by the camouflaged dam?"

"You think so?" Jaubert's excitement was contagious, and I had caught it. "Then we might be close to the Corkindrill anyway!"

"Perhaps."

I stopped. The ground in front of me had shifted and an unintelligent, primeval eye stared up at me.

"Don't move, Captain," whispered Eduzi. "Mr. Croc, he probably won't move. He looks like he's eaten lately. We just have to avoid annoyin' him."

"What annoys him?" I stared back into the crocodile's eyes. It was like staring back into prehistory.

"Well, pretty much everythin' annoys him. What you got to do is hope, pray, and move away. And if he moves towards you, hit him hard behind the eyes."

"Will that kill him?"

"Nope. But it will make him think twice." Eduzi reached out, took my hand, and led me away from the crocodile. "You don't have to worry if you know about crocs. Terrible bad fellers they are when they bite. The muscles that close their jaws are very powerful. Almost two tons for each square inch."

"Two tons per square inch!" I hissed back. "That's insane!"

154

Eduzi nodded, his face profiled by the moon-light. "But the muscles that open their jaws are very weak. You could hold Mr. Croc's mouth closed with just two fingers. If you had just stepped on his jaw and moved on, he couldn't do nothin' about it."

"There's the rest of his body to think of too."

Eduzi gave a quiet laugh. "Yes, that's a big body, you bet. He could toss you off his nose and eat you in two bites. Let's hope you don't have to find out."

By this time, we were on firmer ground, climbing through long grass on the near side of the hill, bent nearly flat by the Undertaker's Breeze. In a few minutes, we had reached the crest of the hill and looked out on an amazing sight beyond.

It looked like a medieval castle, such as you might see in Spain or Portugal. Towers rose at each corner, and tall buildings with windows stood inside the perimeter wall.

"That place," Eduzi breathed, "It used to be a slave camp, you bet."

I frowned. "There's no slave trade any more."

"If you say so, Captain. But this fort, it was built long and long ago, when the white men first came here. This is where the Ashanti people brought their captives, for the white men to buy and take across the ocean. Like those folks there."

155

In a wide open space of grass before the fort stood a large circle of people, many of whom held torches. The flickering orange light lit up a tree in the centre of the circle. It was a huge tree, or perhaps several trees grown together, each trunk shaped curiously like a human body, that seemed to sway in the torchlight, dancing to the hypnotic beat of the drums.

"Iroko!" breathed Aremo.

Eduzi looked sharply at him. "*Igi iroko?*" Aremo nodded. "That tree, Captain, that's the Tree of Forgettin'. When the Ashanti sold their prisoners to the white men, they would lead them seven times around the iroko tree, to make them forget the land of their grandfathers."

Suddenly, the drums stopped, and the cessation of the noise was so abrupt that we all looked down at the circle of people just below us. At the foot of the iroko tree, and flanked by a pair of tall women, stood a new figure. With a great tail and a narrow head, he was some kind of horrid combination of man and crocodile.

"Ombure," I said quietly.

"Ombure," agreed Aremo.

Ombure held out one great claw and crooked a finger. The women moved forward. Tall and muscular, their skin was as dark as ebony, their clothes red and gold. Each wore a cruelly sharp machete on one hip, a Luger on the other. They were like the Amazons from mythology. "Lugers," I said, under my breath. "Of course."

The Amazons seized a man from a crowd at one side of the lawn and led him towards Ombure and the iroko tree. Now I saw that many of the people in the circle were Amazons like Ombure's guards.

"What if he refuses to circle the iroko tree?" I asked Eduzi.

Eduzi shivered, though it was a swelteringly warm night. "Then they will call the iroko man from the tree. That iroko man, you don't want to meet him. He will send you mad. He will make your wits fly away like seed on the wind."

The man gave a cry of anguish, and with a gasp, I saw that he was Kekere.

Ari saw it too. "We have to rescue him," she said.

"What's our plan?" I asked.

Ari held up something that glinted in her hand: the flask of tear-gas she carried concealed in the hollow heel of her boot. "We throw this. We run in. We take Kekere away with us."

157

"*Très magnifique, madame!*" enthused Jaubert. "It is an excellent plan."

"It's almost not a plan at all!" I protested, my voice harsh as I attempted to whisper. "How do we keep the tear-gas out of *our* eyes?"

"We'll have to put up with that as well as we can," returned Ari. "It will be a surprise to all of them, but not to us. We'll be expecting it. And it will disperse quickly—this breeze will blow it away. So it'll be largely gone when we get down there."

Ari quickly told Aremo our plan, and Aremo made a lengthy reply in which the word *Kekere* came up a couple of times. Ari summarized: "He says he knows Kekere does not love him as a brother should, but he does not wish to see him a slave of the white men. That would dishonour his ancestors."

Kekere had completed his first circuit of the iro-ko tree by now. He was screaming and wrenching this way and that between the Amazons.

Ari met my eye. The moon glinted on the flask in her hand. I gave a sigh of defeat. "Well, here we go," I said.

Ari whispered to Assumpta. "Stay here with Archie, where it's safe. Everyone else, when I give the word, we rush down among these people and try to rescue Kekere. Got it?"

There was a chorus of agreement; but Aremo spoke again. Ari listened patiently. By the time Aremo had finished, his brother had completed his second circuit of the Tree of Forgetting. Ombure watched and laughed, his hands on his hips.

"What did he say?"

"He says that only the Child of the Sun can kill Ombure. He can help us, but he can't kill the crocodile god."

"We'll do what we can," I replied, "but I don't know if Archie's up for killing crocodile gods today, or for a while yet."

Ari spoke to Aremo for a moment, then turned back to us. "Are you ready?" We all made the Sign of the Cross. Ari's arm cranked back and the flask shone a moment in the air before it landed on the edge of the circle. There was no noise: the drums drowned it out completely. But instantly, the Amazons in the circle doubled over, coughing, clutching at their eyes. Many of them dropped their torches. Chaos descended upon the space before the iroko tree.

"Let's go!" Ari leaped down from the crest of the hill, and the rest of us followed.

Amazons blundered to and fro. Screams came from all around. The drums had ceased. The tear

159

gas got into my eyes, making them smart, but it was endurable—the Undertaker's Breeze had indeed dispersed the gas. We found Kekere, doubled up and writhing on the ground. Ari stooped over him.

"It's all right," she said. "We've come to take you home." She repeated it in every African language she knew—now quite a lot.

"We'd better get out of here," I suggested. "These Amazons are beginning to recover."

Jaubert and Ari each took hold of one of Kekere's arms and pulled him as gently as they could to his feet. But before we could take a step towards freedom, we heard a voice.

"*Señora!*"

"It's Assumpta." Ari's voice suddenly sounded strangled.

"*Señora!*" repeated Assumpta's voice. "*El bebé, se han llevado el bebé!*"

"They have the baby!" cried Ari. She and I dashed forward, but even as we did, a group of Amazon women, their eyes still streaming from the tear gas, but still very much in possession of themselves, emerged from where Assumpta had been hiding. One of them held Archie. The others held Lugers. One of them tossed Assumpta to the ground before them.

160

"I am sorry, *señora*," wept Assumpta. "I couldn't stop them."

"It's not your fault," said Ari in a voice that was calm, but with an edge under it.

By now more of the Amazons had recovered, and they had surrounded us. They all held Lugers or machetes in their hands. There was no escape, then, for Kekere; and no escape for us.

As the Amazons marched us past the iroko tree and through the gate of the slave camp, I found myself wondering what had become of Aremo and his Crocodile Warriors. Had they even accompanied us on the rescue of Kekere? I couldn't say for sure.

The gate creaked closed behind us and we found ourselves in a wide grassy courtyard. On three sides were two-story buildings, on the third the perimeter wall. More Amazons patrolled the battlements. They held rifles, and watched our progress across the moonlit lawn without particular curiosity.

"McCracken, *regarde!*" Jaubert's voice was shrill with excitement. Outside the largest of the buildings was parked a large vehicle with caterpillar tracks and a glass bubble on the top: the Corkindrill. We exchanged glances. Our adventure had brought us to the right place after all. I was quite amazed by its size. I had read the dimensions, of course, in the blueprints, but it seemed much bigger in real life than in my imagination.

"Even in this was heaven ordinant," whispered Ari, quoting some poet or other no doubt. The Amazon had handed Archie back to her, now that we were safely captured, and his eyes were heavy as he rested his head on her shoulder.

One of the Amazons held open a door and we trooped into the large building. My first impression was of stone and steel. Though a two-story building, the top floor had been removed to accommodate tall gleaming machinery, wheels and presses and levers and pulleys. All the machines were connected by conveyor belts, beside which stood welding irons and screwdrivers and hammers, all stacked neatly for the night. The walls looked down on the machines, as blank as stone could be. A cat-walk ran around where the top floor had been, and the windows had been painted over so that no outside light could come in. The light, harsh and electric, came from naked bulbs suspended from the murky ceiling.

"America has produced very few geniuses," declared an accented voice, and we turned to face a man with longish grey hair and deep circles around his eyes. He had a beetle brow and craggy cheekbones, and he held what looked like a crocodile's head in one hand. The thick tail was draped over his arm. Handing these objects to one of the Amazons, he went on, "One of these geniuses, surely, is Henry Ford, whose inspired assembly lines in Detroit" (he pronounced the word *duh-twa*) "gave me the idea you see here."

"Maurice." Jaubert gave the newcomer a cold nod.

"*Bonjour*, Nicolas," the man returned.

Jaubert turned to us. "*Mes amis*, may I present to you Maurice Strombourg, late captain of the French Navy."

Strombourg's eyes glittered. "Welcome to my factory floor," he said. To Jaubert, he added, "I cannot hide my surprise at seeing you, Nicolas, but perhaps now at last I think you understand."

"I understand that you are a madman," retorted Jaubert. "You would betray your country, your honour, and your God, and for what? German gold?"

Strombourg shook his head sadly, making a clicking sound with his tongue. "Nicolas, Nicolas, how you lack vision! *La France, Allemande, Angleterre*—what could it possibly matter?"

"My apologies, my old friend," replied Jaubert with bitter irony, "I should not have missed the allusion to Henry Ford. How much profit can you make for betraying your country?"

Strombourg raised his eyebrows thoughtfully. "If you wish to put it that way, I suppose you might be correct. But think, Nicolas. What has my country given me? Nothing. For two years France and Germany have been shooting at each other, and neither side is any closer to victory today than when they began. They will destroy each other. And then what? And then what?" He had built to a peak of passion, but paused now and looked on us with what might have been fondness under other circumstances. "Come with me, my friends. I have something to show you."

He led us through the maze of machinery, like a city of shining steel. Part of me admired it—a very large part, I have to admit. Whatever he produced here, he had constructed a very efficient system for doing it.

"Are you familiar with the recent history of l'Afrique?" Strombourg asked as we walked. "For decades, the Germans, the French, and the English have been struggling for control of this continent. When the War began, the French and the English took away the colonies the Germans possessed. But in doing it, they have used up all their resources. They cannot even mend the damage they did fighting the Germans. They will never be able to possess what they have taken. They must return control of the colonies back to the native peoples."

"That's not a bad thing," Eduzi chimed in. "We Africans, why shouldn't we run the lands of our ancestors?"

Strombourg stopped in his tracks. He frowned, as if he'd never heard such an outrageous idea. "Because you are primitive and incompetent," he explained. "Please excuse me, but I do not know you. You seem to be from one of these local tribes. Look at them. They worship crocodile gods, they call in witch doctors to administer *la justice*, they cut themselves barbarically with knives for personal decoration. They are not civilized persons. How could you possibly expect them to rule themselves to any advantage? They need a leader who can rule them all together: one people, one state, one leader."

"And that leader would be you?" I guessed.

Strombourg took one pace towards me. "McCracken, is it not?" I nodded. "I am very pleased to meet you, *monsieur*. I have heard much about you. My congratulations on your elevation to knighthood. I confess, I had not expected to meet you—I did send someone to discourage you from chasing me, but it turns out that he was most inefficient."

"Or my man was just better than he was?" I suggested.

Strombourg's eyes surveyed our group and rested finally on Fritz. He gave a short laugh. "If you say so, *monsieur*. Anyway, my man was expendable, and I am glad to make your acquaintance. As to your question, yes, of course the leader of *l'Afrique Unie* would be myself. I have done all the work. The trouble of obtaining the Corkindrill was mine. The leadership belongs to me. It is my right."

"What can one Corkindrill do to unite Africa?" wondered Ari.

Strombourg studied Ari and Archie closely. I clenched my fists, ready to spring at him if he made any move against either. "*L'enfant, Nicolas—tien?*" Jaubert shook his head. "Ah, then it must be that *l'enfant* belongs to McCracken, and this would be the famous Mademoiselle Bell—Madame McCracken, I should say. Well done, McCracken, she is *très belle*."

"*Ma beauté est pas tes oignons*," said Ari levelly.

Strombourg nodded with a smile. "You speak French, *madame*, even *la français idiomatique—magnifique*! Madame McCracken, and everyone, please allow me the honour of showing you something that I think will impress you." He led us round a corner. There, ranged from one side of the vast room to the other, was a whole rank of Corkindrills, at least twenty of them, all gleaming and fresh from the production line. On the far side of them was a ramp, leading to some water. A wide, dark archway led out of the fortress, presumably to the lagoon. Above the ramp, on the wall, someone had painted a huge map of Africa. All the major cities and rivers were marked on it. Next to it was a clock of very modern design, with clear numbers and a steel case.

"Nicolas," said Strombourg, "you wanted to sail the Corkindrills down the Rhine and the Danube and so attack the Germans from behind. So, you thought, France would win this War. Don't you see what power a fleet of Corkindrills places into the hands of the right man? This continent is networked with rivers, and all the major cities are built on them." He reached for a speaking tube, and talked into it for a few seconds. The language was nothing I recognized.

There came a clattering of footsteps, and suddenly a small army of Amazons had gathered. They stood in a long straight line beside the Corkindrills.

"These are remarkable women, *messieurs et mesdames*," explained Strombourg as the Amazons arrived and paraded. "For three hundred years, these

168

Amazons served the kings of Dahomey. They were noted for their passionate loyalty to the king and their ferocity in battle—far more fierce than any army of men. Finally it was French machine guns that defeated them, and even then, it took three years to subdue them. *Magnifique!* There were very few left in the end. Some of them, if you can believe this, joined a circus run by an American named William Cody."

"Buffalo Bill's Wild West Show," put in Ari.

"*Oui, exactement.* What a degradation! What a humiliation! Some few of them did not wish to submit themselves to such a dishonour, and these I found, and fashioned into my own private army. And now they are loyal to me, and will deliver *l'Afrique* into my hands. Tonight, they leave. And when each of them has taken her position in a river near to a major city, I will give the order, and *Whoosh!* the bombs will begin to fall, and *l'Afrique* will be transformed for ever."

"Why on earth would you want to do that?" I wondered.

"Monsieur McCracken, you surprise me. Has it never occurred to you how full of natural resources this continent is? Gold, copper, ivory, bauxite, diamonds—it is the jewel box of the world! The native

169

people can never unite themselves and take advantage of these natural resources. But now the moment has come, Africa's moment. The European powers fight each other to the death. When the War is over, England and France will be weak, and it will be time for *l'Afrique Unie* to dominate the world."

I ran my hand over one of the conveyor belts. The wheels were perfectly oiled and the rollers spun freely, without any friction. "It's a beautiful assembly line you've built here, Strombourg," I said. "Built by slave labour, I assume?" I shook my head sadly. "Colonial powers change, but the way they enslave the natives is always the same. You're really not so different from the British or the Germans as you would like to think."

Strombourg clicked his tongue several times in sorrowful disapproval. "I should have expected this old-fashioned attitude towards slavery. Madame McCracken, as an American, what do you think? I suggest that the problem with slavery in the United States was that the slave-owners pretended to be Christians. If they had not made that mistake, there would have been no problem, no guilt. The Romans felt no guilt at owning slaves. The Greeks felt no guilt at owning slaves. Only the Americans. Was it not Aristotle who said that some men were natural

170

slaves?" He paused for someone to confirm his as-
sertion. I knew Aristotle had said that, but I wasn't
going to give him the satisfaction of answering.
"Well, I believe it was. Some men are born to be
slaves, owned and ruled by the men of intelligence,
the men of power. And who could be more naturally
slaves than the African peoples? They even sell each
other into slavery. I simply make them more perfectly what they already are."

"So your dream of a united Africa is of Africans
united in slavery?" I asked. "Unity isn't worth much
if that's all it offers."

"How can they be happy trying to be something
they are not?" returned Strombourg with passion.
"McCracken, I confess I am a little disappointed with
you. Your reputation is that of a man of science, an
engineer. But here you are, with all these sentimental ideas." He strolled around the little knot of
adventurers until he came to Ari. He cocked his
head a moment to admire Archie's sleeping cherubic
face. As if suddenly getting a new idea, he snapped
upright and said brightly, "You know, I shouldn't
wonder if all these outmoded ideas didn't come from
some form of religious thought. But it has always
seemed apparent to me that religion is a kind of slavery. The religious person is the slave of God. It's no

different from what I do. Is it wrong to imitate God? Tell me, *s'il vous plaît.*"

Ari licked her lips. She held Archie tightly. She said, "Gods don't die for their slaves."

Strombourg held up his index finger. "But that merely reveals His weakness more. It is time He gave up His ridiculous claim to lordship over the human race. I have seen from my Amazons how selective breeding can improve individual specimens of humanity. Look at them. Are they not *magnifique*? Perfect in physique, in mental fortitude, in discipline. Men have always used selective breeding to improve race horses and dogs. Why not people? Within two or three generations, we can have a race of super men. And then, who has more to do with the creation of men—God or Maurice Strombourg? What do you think, *madame*, would I not then have the right to dispose of men as it pleased me?"

"You think you *are* God," I pointed out.

"No, Monsieur McCracken: God wishes He were me. God's method, always assuming there is one, is extremely random and haphazard. All is left to chance. Strombourg's is streamlined and beautiful. Imagine a world where instead of Corkindrills rolling off a factory floor like this, children did—all perfect children. What could not the human race

172

achieve? Even if there is a God, perhaps He wants us to assert our independence. We have grown beyond childhood. It is time for us to live our own lives."

"But you don't want Africans to live their own lives," I said. "You want them to serve you."

Strombourg shrugged. "There must be hierarchy," he said. He looked up at the clock. "But Time, she runs. I must be about changing the course of history." He reached out and tickled Archie under the chin. Ari shrank away from him as Archie stirred. "A beautiful child." Strombourg's voice was so low I could barely hear him. "Strong, beautiful, and intelligent—a combination of traits from both mother and father. With the proper education, he might be my worthy successor."

"I think we can educate Archie perfectly well, thank you," said Ari, still backing away.

Strombourg's eyes flicked up at his Amazons, and his hand moved sharply. Instantly, a flurry of motion erupted among us: one Amazon seized Ari by the upper arms while another snatched away Archie and passed him, awake now and beginning to wail, to Strombourg.

Ari screamed and lunged for Strombourg. One of the Amazons struck her across the face.

I roared with fury and rushed forward, reaching for my son. But Amazons closed in on me. I saw the butt of a Luger hurtling towards my head, saw a flash of light, and then knew nothing more.

CHAPTER 15
TROUBLE AT THE FACTORY

All the images of that horrible moment rushed into my mind the moment I awoke: Strombourg with Archie, the implacable faces of the Amazons, the explosion of pain in my head as the butt of the Luger crashed into it.

Darkness surrounded me, and the first thing I noticed was actually the smell: a terrible stench of many human beings kept in a poorly ventilated space for too long. Then I knew I was lying among filth, and my wrists and ankles were pinched; iron shackles bit into my flesh, not deeply, but constantly. Slowly, my sight came back to me, but it was almost completely dark.

I was in a small, dirty room, manacled to the wall with iron chains. My companions sat among the filth with me. Through the single window, high in the wall, shone the half moon.

"Herr McCracken," said Fritz's voice, with concern, "your head, does it still hurt?"

"Yes, a bit," I replied. "Archie?"

Ari's chains rattled as she stood. "Strombourg," she said. "Strombourg has—has our baby."

175

I got, wobbling, to my feet and turned her to face me. The light was faint, but I got her to look into my face. "We'll get him back," I assured her. "Whatever it takes, we'll get him back. What's our situation?"

"We are all chained." Jaubert's voice. "Through that door is the dormitory of the slaves who work in Strombourg's factory. This room is very small—it might have been a storage room originally. You have been unconscious about one quarter of an hour."

"You were right, Mac." Ari again. "You were—right. We should have—should have never brought—Archie—on this trip."

"Nonsense," I replied brusquely. "The laddie has to have his first adventure. You still have those TNT charges?"

"That we have already discussed," said Jaubert. "We cannot blow the door off its hinges. The room is too small."

"The TNT is for Strombourg's factory." I tested the manacles on my wrists. There was nothing doing with them.

"Is there anybody here who can pick a lock?" wondered Eduzi.

"There's one." Actually, there were at least two. I knew how and so did Ari. But it was time to illuminate our situation a little, and I was probably only the second-best lock-pick on our expedition anyway. "There's one among us who can pick a lock, isn't there, Assumpta?"

After a long pause, Assumpta said, "*Si, señor.* I do not know how it is you know, but I can pick a lock."

"Assumpta? You can pick a lock?" Ari's voice was somewhere between amazement and admiration.

We all heard the jangle of chains falling to the floor, and Assumpta rose from her captivity.

"It's necessary in her line of business," I explained.

"What line of business?" asked Ari. "Nannying?"

Assumpta moved over to Ari, bent over her wrists and ankles, and in a moment her chains fell away and she stood there, free and rubbing her wrists.

"I am a jewel thief, *señora.* Becoming nanny for you enabled me to make a perfect getaway at just the right time. My professional name—you might have heard of it—is The Jewel."

There was a long silence in the gloomy dungeon. Then Ari said, "Well, you're a fine nanny as well."

177

With a smile, Assumpta quickly released us all.

When our chains lay in little heaps, shining coldly in the weak moonlight, we crept over to the door and opening it I peeked through the gap. The sound of snoring greeted me, along with a wretched miasma of human stench. I could see rows of people stretched out on mattresses, their forms softened by patched blankets. Strombourg's workforce slept fitfully, rolling in their sleep, mumbling, grinding their teeth. Did they dream of rivets and welding irons and wing-nuts? I wondered. Closing the door softly, I turned to Jaubert and whispered, "What's beyond the dormitory?"

"The factory floor."

I nodded. "Right then. There are still a few things I need to know. Jaubert, how far can Strombourg have got in the Corkindrill?"

"Not far yet," he replied. "A mile, perhaps one mile and one half."

"So perhaps as far as the end of the lagoon—the dam?"

"Not yet," replied Jaubert. "But he will get to it soon, and that will lead him out into another very large lagoon, from which rivers lead all over Africa. If he gets through the dam, finding him will be very difficult indeed."

178

"Here's the plan, then," I said. "Jaubert, you and I will follow Strombourg in the prototype Corkindrill parked outside, sink his Corkindrill and rescue Archie. Ari, you use your TNT charges to blow up the factory. Eduzi, Assumpta and Fritz, you release the slaves and get them out of here before the factory blows."

"I'm coming with you." Ari's voice did not sound human. It was a snarl, like a tiger's, and I knew there would be no gainsaying her.

"Mac." I noticed that Assumpta's voice had lost its South American accent. There was something of California in it, I thought, perhaps around San Francisco. "Give me the TNT. I can blow up the factory—I've done things like that before."

I nodded. "Ari, let her have the charges." Ari reached down to the heels of her boots and passed the TNT charges to Assumpta.

"Those fuses are about thirty seconds," she said.

"Is your name really Assumpta?" I asked.

She nodded. "Assumpta Bevan. Born in Patagonia, raised in Los Gatos, California. I hope you won't use that information against me." She smiled in the darkness.

"Of course not. Place the TNT against the fuel tanks or something like that—there must be fuel for

179

the Corkindrills somewhere. Wait until the slaves are all out before you light the fuses. But make sure you have an escape route first."

"I always do."

I grinned. "Of course!" I turned to the others. "We'll all meet where the Path of Ombure came out, right?" Everyone nodded. "Then, if everyone knows what he's doing, let's go."

I cast open the door and we plunged in among the crowded bodies. We picked our way slowly between them, Eduzi and Fritz staying behind to awaken them as soon as we were out on the factory floor.

A double line of yellow light showed around the door that led to the factory floor. I leaned on it enough to open it a few inches, and looked through the crack. For a moment I blinked—after the darkness of the dungeon and the dormitory, the tungsten floodlights were blinding. But when my eyes adjusted, I could see the conveyor belt running almost as far as the door to the outside. About five yards short of the door, the conveyor belt turned back on itself. It provided us with cover part way to the door, but there was a short space we had to cross with nothing behind which we could hide.

Voices echoed from the far side of the factory, and I could hear the engine of a Corkindrill.

180

"The Corkindrills, McCracken," said Jaubert. "They must be launching them. Most of them must still be in this building. When Mademoiselle Assumpta blows up the factory—*bang!*—up will go the Corkindrills too." He grinned. "I wish I could see it."

"God be with you, Assumpta," I said.

"And with you, Mac." Assumpta gave a smile and was gone. The rest of us filed out from the dormitory towards the cover of the conveyor belt. Behind us, we heard the first stirrings of the slaves as Eduzi and Fritz began to awaken them from their uneasy slumber.

We ran at a crouch, keeping our heads below the top of the conveyor belt. The Amazons at the far side of the factory would not be able to see us until we reached the open space before the door. But about halfway to our objective, I couldn't resist raising my head a little to see what was going on. Amazons still stood to attention in front of the rank of Corkindrills, but one of the vehicles was lumbering towards the ramp, smoke puffing from its exhaust pipes. The instruments of world domination were underway. I lowered my head and we dashed to the end of the conveyor belt. The open space lay before us, in full view of the Amazons launching the Corkindrills. Worse, the door was guarded by another Amazon, a rifle slung over her shoulder, a machete hanging at her side.

Ari looked at us over her shoulder. "What are you waiting for? Archie's out there." And out she rushed across the open space.

"*Vive l'aventure!*" said Jaubert, and ran after her.

The Amazon was watching the Corkindrills, and Ari had crossed half the distance to her before she noticed anything was amiss. Then her features seemed to spring apart, as if exploding: her eyebrows shot up, her jaw dropped. She let the rifle slip from her shoulder to the floor, and her fingers closed around the hilt of the machete.

Too late.

Ari sprang like a cat, knocking her down. I saw Ari's elbow jerk upwards, and her fist crashed into the Amazon's face. The guard was still. Ari took up the machete and threw open the door. I picked up the rifle as I passed.

Behind us, I heard shouts of alarm, not quite drowned out by the noise of the Corkindrills' engines. Gunshots rang out. I paused and turned back. The slaves had begun to emerge from the dormitory, and a battle was beginning. But I could not stay for it, and ran after Ari.

The prototype Corkindrill was still outside in the courtyard, some yards away. But an Amazon stood on top of it, her rifle leveled at us. Other Amazons were running up from their stations on the walls. In a moment, we were surrounded by Amazons, all armed with rifles and machetes.

The Amazon on the Corkindrill said something and laughed. She knew she had us at her mercy. One of the Amazons surrounding us cocked the rifle and aimed at my head. I made the Sign of the Cross and committed my soul into God's care.

But the gunshot did not come. Instead, the Amazon with the rifle gave a gasp and staggered forward, dropping her weapon. An arrow protruded from between her shoulder blades. Immediately, confusion descended upon the courtyard. Another Amazon fell to an arrow from an unseen bowman.

We took advantage of the situation at once. Ari launched herself up the side of the Corkindrill and shoved the Amazon unceremoniously to the ground. I found the steel rungs on the stern of the Corkindrill and climbed up on top.

"*Jeka lo!*" came a voice from the darkness, and a moment later a wave of Crocodile Warriors swarmed over the Amazons, Aremo waving cheerfully to me. I grinned and waved back. All the time

183

we had been in Strombourg's factory, he and his men had been infiltrating the slave camp!

I dived for the Corkindrill's hatch and tumbled through it, landing in an ungainly pile on the floor. Above me, Ari slammed the hatch closed and sealed it.

"*Seigneur*," prayed Jaubert, "I pray this vehicle may be fully fueled." Making the Sign of the Cross, he called out: "McCracken, would you please to start the engine?"

As large as it was from the outside, the Corkindrill was not spacious on the inside. In the middle of it rose the housing for the engine, and I had to squeeze between that and the retracted 75mm gun. But there, between the two rear-facing seats, was the crank, and I threw my back into it and turned it a few times. The engine sputtered a couple of times, and then filled the confined space with its roar.

"*Merci!*" came Jaubert's faint voice as we lumbered off across the courtyard. Once again, I squeezed past the gun, noting the neat row of 75mm shells, and took my seat beside Jaubert. I could see nothing of our progress, because the narrow vision-slit was on the driver's side.

"McCracken." Jaubert jabbed his forefinger through the forward slit. "The gates are closed."

184

I understood at once. The Corkindrill thundered towards the lock gates, its wheels squealing and the caterpillar tracks clanking. I pushed open the hinged splinter shields in the vehicle's outer casing—they were sealed with rubber, and I could feel the slight pop as the seal was broken—and trundled the gun out, throwing the lock to keep it in place. Taking one of the shells, I slotted it into the breech and peered down the sight. I cranked a handle. The barrel swung downwards. I cranked another handle, and the crosshairs slid sideways to the gate. I moved aside and yanked on the firing pin.

The explosion was terrific, and shook the whole frame of the Corkindrill. Ari reached out to steady herself against one of the bulkheads. When the breech had returned to the firing position, I looked down the sight once more. The gates were wrapped in a mantle of smoke, eerily lit up by the torches and moonlight.

"Bravo, *monsieur!*" cried Jaubert. "A fine shot!"

The Corkindrill's tracks crunched on the debris that marked the place where the gates had been, and immediately the vehicle shook and the engine's pitch whined.

"What's happened?" Ari leaned forward, trying to see past Jaubert through the forward slit. "Are we stuck?"

Jaubert switched to a higher gear. "We are stuck on the wreckage of the gates, *madame*, but we should be free in a moment." His brow was wrinkled as he wrestled with levers and the steering wheel, his foot pumping at one pedal and then another.

I climbed up into the observation dome and peered down at the wreckage. "Come on, Jaubert," I said under my breath, as the Corkindrill struggled. I could see the caterpillar tracks flying towards me, tossing bits and pieces of debris into the air.

Something struck the glass canopy behind my head, and I turned to see that something had cracked it—a bullet. A fight was going on in the courtyard, between Aremo's men and the slaves on the one hand, and the Amazons on the other. I could see the muzzle flashes from the Lugers and rifles, but could hear nothing over the Corkindrill's engine.

The Corkindrill shuddered, skewed to the port, and heaved itself up onto the wreckage. She was free! Heaving a sigh of relief, I dropped back into the seat beside Jaubert.

"I knew it would not take long," said Jaubert grimly. "We made the angle of the prow oblique so that it could manoeuvre over trenches."

"Clever," I remarked.

"Can't you go faster, Nicolas?" Ari's knuckled were white as she grasped the back of his seat.

"Regrettably no, *madame*," replied Jaubert. "Six kilometres per hour is our maximum, though under the water she is a great deal faster."

I couldn't stand it any more, and climbed once again into the observation dome. To our left, the iroko tree rumbled past at an achingly-slow six kilometres per hour; on our right, the lost lagoon stretched out in the moonlight, as if asleep.

Except that two boat-like objects plied across its glassy surface.

"I can see two Corkindrills on the lagoon!" I shouted down to Jaubert and Ari.

"Are they in range?"

"I think so. A difficult shot, though."

"You're not going to fire on them?" Ari's voice rose in alarm. "Archie is in one of them."

Most likely the lead one, I thought, watching as the deceptively peaceful little objects moved slowly across the shining waters. But Ari was right—it wasn't worth the risk.

"Let's just catch up with them." Ari's pale face was turned up towards me. "They'll have to slow down when they reach the dam."

"And then what?" I asked. "Do you have a plan?"

Ari nodded. "Hit them until they give him back."

"I might hit them even after they give him back," I said grimly.

At that moment, there came a tremendous roar from behind us, and the whole lagoon was lit up with an orange glow. The Corkindrill rocked a little. I spun around to look behind us.

"What was that?" asked Ari.

"The factory blew up." A great, glowing cloud rose from the slave camp. Bits and pieces of debris thumped to the ground all around us. "God bless Assumpta!"

The stars grew dim as the smoke expanded outwards. The golden cloud began to disperse, but fires raged within the slave camp. The walls, shattered now like the walls of Douala, stood silhouetted against the flames. The iroko tree also stood, dark and knotted, against the brightness of the burning ruins.

"I hope they all got clear," said Ari, so low I could barely hear her over the thunder of the engine.

I strained my eyes to see through the weird landscape. And there, under the iroko tree, stood some figures—many of them, in fact. One of them—I would have wagered a large sum it was Eduzi—held up a torch, and a moment later the iroko tree was a ball of fire. In its light, I could see a crowd of workers, Crocodile Warriors, even Amazons, striding side by side from the ruins of the slave camp.

I couldn't help smiling. "Africans united," I said with quiet satisfaction.

"Hold on, everyone!" Jaubert shouted. "Here is rough ground!"

At once, we plunged in among sand dunes, starting pale birds from their sleep and into the night air. The water of the lagoon was very close. I dropped from the observation dome and down to the starboard gun, Ari crouching behind me and peering through the opening eagerly.

For a moment, everything seemed to go still. We had entered the water, and no longer made our way across firm ground. Jaubert flipped a large switch above his head. I heard grinding gears behind us, then the slow thumping of a propeller getting underway. The Corkindrill seemed to surge forward. Jaubert had been right—she was faster in the water. Some water shipped in through the gun port, splashing across my knees.

Ahead of us, I could see the two Corkindrills, lit up by the fires from the slave camp. I slotted another shell into the breech of the 75mm gun.

"What are you doing?" Ari's voice was high-pitched.

Before I could reply, I heard a muffled report and saw a muzzle flash from the nearer of the Corkindrills. An explosion nearby rocked our vessel.

"*Mon Dieu!*" cried Jaubert. Water was seeping in and puddling around his feet. My eyes scanned the controls. We could ship several more inches' worth of water before it reached any of the electrics and shorted us out.

But now the waves from the nearby explosion reached us. We rocked from side to side, and more water splashed in through the gun-port. I reported the fact to Jaubert.

Jaubert said something under his breath, then aloud added: "This is a tank that swims, McCracken, not a battleship. We did not design her for combat on the waves."

Another muzzle flash. The round screamed overhead. The roar of the explosion came from be-

190

hind, and the waves once more rocked us back and forth. More water slopped in through the gun-port.

"McCracken," pleaded Jaubert, "would it be at all possible for you to disable the nearer of the Corkindrills?"

"I'm on it," I said, snapping the breech shut over the shell.

"Wait." Ari's hand was on my arm. "Archie might be in that one."

"I'm not going to blow it up or sink it, just disable it."

"Oh." Ari wrung her hands as the crank went round and round and the muzzle dropped. The cross-hairs passed the Corkindrill's exhausts. They were targeted on the foamy wake churned up by the propellers. I turned the crank a fraction more.

"How accurate are these guns, Jaubert?" I asked.

"They are the best available to the *Armée Française*," replied Jaubert. "We had them from the Government Arsenal in Bourges."

I paused a moment. A slight miscalculation could be disastrous. But there were no huge waves, as at sea, to throw off my aim.

"Mac," said Ari.

But even as I hesitated, the other Corkindrill's rear gun fired. This time the round landed ten yards from us, and the explosion threw gallons of water through the gun-port, so that Ari and I choked and spluttered.

"Ari," I said softly, my fingers closed about the firing cord, "one more shot like that and Archie will be an orphan. Trust me." I pulled the cord.

The boom rattled my brain and my ears, and the Corkindrill rocked. The breech jolted backwards, spitting out the empty shell. Ari and I craned forward. A plume of water erupted from the lagoon right behind the nearer of the Corkindrills—the round had exploded in the water behind our enemy, and not against the body of the vehicle. It was just what I had planned.

"More luck than accuracy," I said with satisfaction.

"You missed," said Ari.

But even as she said it, a wide pool of oil began to spread out from the stern of the Corkindrill. It began to peel away from its course in a wide arc. "I've ruptured its fuel tank and damaged its rudder. I'm sure it rattled the crew, but it won't have killed anyone." Ari leaned forward and kissed me on the cheek.

But now, I saw, the lead Corkindrill had reached the far end of the lagoon, and had come to a stop below a short cliff, about fifteen feet in height, covered with vines.

"We've got him now!"

But Jaubert shook his head. "Remember, McCracken, how I told you of the dam that separated this lagoon from another, larger lagoon?"

"That's a dam?" I whistled. "Nice camouflage."

The hatch in the top of the Corkindrill opened, and a head emerged, followed by the lithe body of Maurice Strombourg. He reached out for some foliage, which he thrust aside to reveal iron rungs. Nimbly, he swung himself up these and onto the top of the dam. Casting aside more vines, he revealed what looked like a set of levers. They looked like the ones I had constructed to operate the bridge back in the Honduras.

"There must be some kind of sluice gate," I said, "so he can get out of this lagoon and into the other one. No doubt all the rivers feed into the large lagoon."

A tremor ran through the Corkindrill, and I held out a hand to steady myself. "What was that?"

Jaubert pointed. "We are under attack, McCracken, from a new enemy." Peering through the gun-port, I saw what looked like a log in the water. Lines of raised bumps were tipped with orange

193

light from the burning slave camp. The log rose, and I saw a line of pale teeth. "These crocodiles," said Jaubert, "they are fierce in guarding their territory, *n'est-ce pas*?"

A dull boom sounded, and fire flashed from the enemy Corkindrill. The overhead shriek of the round was too close for comfort. "It won't take them long to get a bearing on us at this range," I observed.

We were so close that I could see the muzzle of the Corkindrill's gun cranking downwards. Fifteen rounds per minutes—that was what a team of six could fire from one of these guns in the field. But the Corkindrill had a smaller crew, and their captain was on top of the dam, not in the vessel itself. I counted slowly . . . eight . . . nine . . . ten . . .

Flash and boom. Smoke curled from the barrel of the gun. A force like a train wreck slammed into the starboard side of our Corkindrill, tossing me from my seat and against a bulkhead. Ari screamed.

The valiant Corkindrill now listed heavily to port, and more water poured in. Slowly, she turned over on her side, and then kept going. The glass canopy slid under the water, which began to ooze in through the crack made earlier. We all tumbled against the ceiling as the vessel completed its capsize.

"Come on!" cried Ari, reaching for the clasps on the canopy. Together, she and Jaubert pushed it open and, one by one, we slipped through into the lagoon.

For a moment, I found myself in a murky world, unsure which way was up. Something punched me in the chest, and I was aware of a pair of malevolent eyes staring into my own.

I had to think quickly. What was it Eduzi had said? I saw a line of teeth, half an inch wide, appear all around the snout of the crocodile. Quickly, I reached out and grabbed the beast's snout with my hand, clamping the jaws shut. The crocodile's eyes widened, and its tail lashed. But I had gained the moment I needed. I kicked with my feet and a moment later pulled myself out of the water, joining Ari and Jaubert on the shore of the lagoon.

All three of us stood, dripping, below the dam, looking up at the dark outline of Strombourg above us. One of his hands was upon the sluice gate, which he had raised over an opening in the dam like the portcullis of a medieval castle.

"Well done, Nicolas," he said, "and well done, McCracken. You have destroyed my fortress and my plan. But you are without transport. You will not catch me."

Strombourg leaped down onto the deck of the remaining Corkindrill. The sluice gate was open and, just before the hatch closed, we heard Archie crying from within. The screw turned, and the Corkindrill began to move through the gate.

CHAPTER 16
AN AMPHIBIOUS SOLUTION

For a few seconds, none of us moved. We were frozen, as if in ice. The sound of Archie's shrill cry still seemed to echo in my ears. And it was that sound that stirred me.

Somehow, Ari had managed to carry the machete from the wreck of the Corkindrill. My hand darted out and seized it. She was so surprised that she cried out, but released the machete. I leaped for the iron rungs and clambered up them to the top of the dam, my fingers slipping on the slick iron. In a moment I was standing where, just now, Strombourg had lorded it over us.

The Corkindrill was almost halfway through the sluice gate. I could see Strombourg's face in profile through the glass of the observation dome. The glass had some imperfections, and it magnified his craggy cheek-bones and his beetle brow. Seeing me he turned and saluted.

The sluice gate was still suspended above the dam. It was wrought from iron—wood would have rotted long ago—with sharp points at the bottom that presumably fitted into sockets under the water.

It was held up by a length of chain that snaked through a pulley and down to the winch by which Strombourg had raised it.

I heaved the machete over my head, and with all the strength of a distressed father brought the edge crashing into the chain. The links popped apart. The sluice gate rattled and fell. It crashed into the Corkindrill's stern deck, smashing through steel plates like teeth through cheese. The bows of the Corkindrill rose a few inches; the stern dropped. Strombourg darted a glance over his shoulder, saw what had happened, and gunned the engine. The iron teeth of the sluice gate drove deeper into the Corkindrill, lodging it still more firmly. A terrible grinding noise came from its hull as the spikes tore holes in the armour plating. The bows tipped up more, and water swirled through the holes. The engine gave a gurgle, then coughed and died.

Strombourg realized what had happened. He glared at me with a look of perfect hatred, then seized something from inside the Corkindrill, threw open the observation dome, and jumped out onto the top of the dam, a machete in his hand.

"Give me back my son," I said, "and I'll let you go where you want."

"I shall go where I want anyway, McCracken," he replied, "but I will kill you first."

Leaping forward, he swung the machete at me. I didn't see it coming—only a blur of steel and the hiss of the edge slicing the air. Without thinking, I raised my own machete and the two met in mid-air, inches from my face. The hammer-and-anvil sound of the blades rang out across the waters on either side of the dam.

Strombourg lunged again, his attack coming at my right side and then my left. I put up a ragged defence, blocking each attack clumsily. The ferocity of his attack surprised me, though, and I stepped backwards along the spine of the dam. Then came another attack, and another, and another. Each one pushed me back along the dam, towards the forest, away from Archie.

Strombourg paused, his eyes watching me keenly. They glinted in the orange glow from the fires. I was grateful for the lull, though I knew it would get worse when the fight resumed. So far, I had blocked every one of his lunges, and I knew I could keep that up for some time. But I had to take the offensive at some point, and at least disable him. If I could draw him into making a mistake, perhaps by taunting him or—

From inside the Corkindrill came the sound of Archie crying, and I completely forgot what I had been planning. Strombourg snapped the blade of his machete at me, and my response was slow. The tip of his machete grazed my stomach, and I felt the hot pain of the wound and a warm dampness sticking to my shirt. I grunted, and fell back out of range of his blade, clutching my wound with my left hand. It was only slight, but messy.

"*Touché!*" Strombourg laughed. "You see, McCracken, how fatherhood has weakened your defence!"

"You really talk a lot, don't you?" I answered, and swung my machete at him. He parried it easily, and followed up with a diagonal slash. I blocked it and fell back another step. Twice more he tried to slash at my head, but I defended myself, retreating each time. I was getting tired now—my arm ached with holding the machete up so long, and I was sweating and panting heavily with the exertion. I made a desperate attempt at an attack, but Strombourg avoided it with ease. Once again, he attacked. The blades flashed in the moonlight, and our machetes sang a grim metallic song as I was pressed towards the forest behind me and the water's edge. My foot slipped on some mud, and my arm flew out for balance. I snatched a glance behind me—right into the dull, primordial eyes of a crocodile. Strombourg pressed his advantage, slashing at my leg. The razor-sharp blade sliced through my flesh and into my shin-bone, and the pain shook my body as if pistons were pounding my nerves. Crying out in agony, I dropped to my other knee. My machete went flying from my hand and I heard it splash into the lagoon. Blood flowed from my wounds into the mud.

Strombourg panted as he stood above me. He took a couple of steps forward, a looming tower. I was defenceless and at his mercy; I had lost. The last blow would come at any moment, and I would be dead. I didn't even have the strength to make the Sign of the Cross.

"Who do you think you are, McCracken?" demanded Strombourg. "I learned to fight from the Amazon Warriors of Dahomey." The machete swung loosely from his hand. "From whom did you learn?"

"From drunks in Aberdeen," I grunted back at him. It was all posturing, of course. I had no resources of strength or skill left. All I could do was pray, "Into your hands I commend my spirit, Lord."

A marvelous stillness came over me, and I was suddenly aware of the scene around me in a way I had never been before. I saw the dark smear of my own blood along the edge of Strombourg's machete. I heard the chilling gurgle of the crocodile behind me. I saw a bird, perhaps the one our Corkindrill had startled earlier, winging its way over the dam to freedom.

A human body is like a machine. The arms are levers, the joints the fulcrums, the muscles pulleys. The feet are inclined planes, the teeth simple wedges, the spinal column a screw. Like any machine, apply force to the right point and it will go in the desired direction.

"*Adieu*, McCracken," said Strombourg, and raised the machete high over his head.

I applied effort to the fulcrum of my knee, and rose towards Strombourg. One hand darted out and seized his elbow, shaking it so that the machete spiraled uselessly from his fingers. The other hand, balled into a fist, slammed into his stomach so that his body doubled up around the fulcrum of his lower back. He took a step backwards, slipped on the mud, and toppled sideways.

I saw a great pair of jaws open, and rows of teeth showed bright in the moonlight. The jaws closed

202

again with a force of two tons per square inch, and Strombourg cried out. I tried to help him, but my wounded leg gave out and I sprawled onto the top of the dam. A grey body, ridged like a log, slid forward over Strombourg, and the crocodile and its awful burden vanished into the lagoon.

Jaubert and Ari, Archie in her arms, came hurrying up. She must have rescued him while I had been fighting Strombourg.

"Maurice!" Jaubert looked helplessly at the flurry of underwater movement. Then ripples extended outwards, echoed from the shore, and were gone. Jaubert made the Sign of the Cross. "*Requiem aeternam dona ei, Domine,*" he said.

"*Et lux perpetua luceat ei,*" Ari and I responded.

"*Requiescat in pace,*" we all said together. "Amen."

* * *

Ari bound my wounds and splinted my leg, and Jaubert gave me his shoulder to lean on as we made our way back to our rendezvous point. We found Fritz and Eduzi waiting for us at the mouth of the tunnel.

"Where's Assumpta?" I asked.

203

"Hasn't got back yet, Captain," replied Eduzi.

"McCracken, *regarde*." Jaubert had stooped to collect his diving gear, only to find that the front porthole of his helmet was covered with red wax, impressed with the image of a dragon and the words *The Jewel*. Frowning, he picked it up, and a shining object flashed through the air, landing with a soft thump on the earth. It was the statue of Kinich Ahau, to which was tied a small piece of neatly-folded paper. Ari unfolded it and read the contents.

My Very Dear Friends,

I've stolen this from two different chieftains, and I think that's enough fun. Please return it to its rightful owner, which is not the British Government, by the way.

I'm sorry to have deceived you all, but I needed to get away from the British Honduras quickly, and hope you won't hold it against me. I have come to love you all very much, particularly little Archie. Please give him a hug from me, and tell him his *Querida* will miss him very much until we meet again.

Yours Ever,
Assumpta Montero (The Jewel).

Nobody spoke for a while, but we listened to the chirping of the insects along the shore of the lost lagoon. At last, I sighed. "Well," I said, "I don't think we've heard the last of The Jewel."

* * *

It took us the best part of a week to get to Accra, the capital of the Gold Coast, where I was needlessly hospitalized for a further week on account of the machete-chop I had taken to the leg. There, we composed a short message to Aymerich, and caught a ride on another cruiser of the Royal Navy, which deposited us back in Douala. When we stepped onto the wharf, rain was coming down in sheets, lightning flashing and thunder rolling. Eduzi looked up into the slate-grey clouds.

"Yes, Captain, it looks like the rainy season began, you bet." Turning to me, he thrust out his hand, which I shook heartily. "It's been a wild adventure," he said. "Next time you're needin' a guide, you let Eduzi know, all right?"

"You're my first choice, Eduzi," I said. And, grinning widely, he was gone.

An army car took us first to the hotel, where Ari, Fritz and Archie disembarked, and then on to the

Government Building. There, Aymerich listened patiently to our report of the loss of the Corkindrill and the madness of Maurice Strombourg. When we had finished, he said, "The Republic of France thanks you, gentlemen. This operation was gallantly carried out."

"In spite of its loss," said Jaubert, "the Corkindrill performed well, *mon Général*, and I have many ideas for improvements in the design. May I assume that production will begin soon?"

Aymerich's smile was tinged with sadness. "Alas, *mon ami*, I regret not." He gave a sigh and sat back in his chair. Stroking his beard reflectively for a moment, he went on, "Currently, France insists on investing all its war budget in land-tanks and aeroplanes." Jaubert looked deflated. Aymerich hurried on: "The men who make these decisions, Nicolas, they often lack imagination. The Corkindrill is a risk."

"*Mais las guerre est le risque,*" responded Jaubert; then, remembering I had no French, he added, "War is always a risk, *Général.*"

Aymerich nodded. "Yes, I understand that; I am a soldier, after all. But the risk is to men's lives. It is the money that these men are unwilling to risk."

"I think I understand." Jaubert's lips were twisted into a bitter smile as he rose from his seat. "What I do not understand is why we should have to risk our lives thwarting the plans of a man like Strombourg, when the men running the *Armée Française* are no different from him."

"I do not like this, *monsieur*," replied Aymerich, "but soldiers have always carried out the wishes of men of . . . shall we say of malleable morality?"

"But if our leaders will not lead us morally, who can?" Jaubert's words came out as a torrent.

I smiled. I was thinking of the bridge I had helped build in the forest of the British Honduras. I had helped the villagers because the British police force could not. "I don't have to be here," I said, leaning on my walking-stick to get up.

Aymerich held up a hand. "Please remain, Monsieur McCracken. There is still a small amount of business I must discuss with you."

"Will you need me at all, *Général*?" asked Jaubert. Aymerich shook his head. "Then I bid you *adieu*. McCracken, shall I see you at the hotel?"

"I'll be there presently." Jaubert nodded and left me alone with Aymerich. The general reached into a desk and pulled out two envelopes. I smiled again.

It seemed like a repeat of the scene . . . I couldn't even guess how long ago . . . in Belize City.

"Monsieur McCracken." Aymerich handed me one of the envelopes, which was addressed in French. "You have acquitted yourself with great gallantry, and the Republic of France commends you most highly. Should Capitaine Strombourg have succeeded in his plans, disaster would surely have followed for Africa and the world. And, of course, as a citizen of France he would have been a very great discredit to her. As it is, the world will know him only as a war hero."

I nodded. "That's how some heroes are made." I still hadn't opened the envelope, but I could guess at its contents.

"That letter," explained Aymerich, "is your honourable discharge, with distinction, from the Armed Forces of France." He stood to attention and, almost under a compulsion, I followed suit. General Joseph Aymerich raised his right hand and saluted me. Then, as is the French custom, he kissed me on either cheek. "My deepest admiration, *monsieur*, and, might I add . . . my envy."

"Your envy?"

"*Oui. Monsieur*, you fight this War as it should be fought, with courage and honour and morality.

208

You are accountable to no politician. You are free to do right, to do the will of God. Only you can do this. I hope that you can help Nicolas Jaubert understand this also."

I couldn't help smiling. "Nicolas is a quick learner," I said. "I think it won't be too long before he understands."

Aymerich held out the other envelope. "This is a communication from Brigadier-General Dobell."

I tore it open and scanned it. "It seems *HMS Amphitrite* is still in the vicinity and ready to carry me and my family to England so I can fill my appointment with Vickers-Armstrong."

"Will you accept the offer?"

"Perhaps," I said, "but I have a duty to perform first. I have to take something back to its rightful owners, and the *Amphitrite* won't be able to help me."

Aymerich narrowed his eyes. "Do you have appropriate transport?"

"Oh yes. I cabled a friend of mine. If he can tear himself away from his coffee plantation for a little while, he can take me back to Mexico for a short time."

"Perhaps for you, *monsieur*," said Aymerich, a glint in his eye, "the adventure is not over."

I slipped both letters into my pocket. "Oh, you know the McCrackens," I said. "Adventure just seems to find us."

"So it is with all men, *monsieur. Adieu.* I have been privileged to know you, and hope we shall meet again soon."

Aymerich had laid on another motor-car for me, and the rain hammered on the roof all the way back to the hotel. We were delayed a few minutes because the road was blocked by labourers who were moving timber to a site where they were rebuilding damage wrought by the naval bombardment, all those months ago. I sighed. Eduzi would have known an alternate route.

When I reached our room, I found Jaubert already sitting looking out of the window. He was sipping a Cognac and studying the statue of Kinich Ahau. Ari was nowhere in sight.

"Madame McCracken," said Jaubert in a hushed voice, "is with young Master Archimedes."

"I'll go and say hello." I pushed open the door to find Ari leaning over Archie's crib, folding the blankets up to his chin. She flashed a smile at me as I entered, and we stood for a while, admiring the miracle that had been brought into our lives, asleep now under the cool of the ceiling fan.

"Look at him," I whispered. "You'd never think his life was in danger recently."

Ari squeezed my hand. "Babies' lives are in danger ten or twelve times a day, and their mothers and fathers save them without even thinking about it. We just had the good fortune to be able to save his life from a megalomaniac intent on world domination."

"We have all the luck." We went back out into the lounge, to find that Fritz had brought us all drinks. "Hello." I peered through the window. The rain had stopped, and blue skies were beginning to prevail. From our vantage point, we could see the harbour, and a familiar shape was chugging up alongside the wharf. "The *Fortune of Serpents*."

"*Quoi*?" asked Jaubert.

Ari was smiling. "A ship owned by a very dear friend of ours. He'll take us to Mexico, and then to London."

"While I . . . " Jaubert paused. "What will I do, I wonder? I have no Corkindrill project to occupy me."

"No Corkindrill project?" Ari was surprised.

"*Oui, madame*. It has been cancelled. They wish to fund other weapons."

"Oh Nicolas, I'm so sorry."

211

"Perhaps it is for the best," reasoned Jaubert. "Such a weapon in the hands of politicians might be worse than Strombourg. One must consider, what would one do with the Corkindrill after the War has finished? I was thinking only of ending the War more quickly, but I should have been thinking about the kind of men who would be using the Corkindrill. Perhaps then I might not have trusted Strombourg so completely."

"Come with us," I urged him. "Come to Mexico and to England. There are still things we can do."

"I shall think about your proposal," replied Jaubert. "In fact, I believe I shall accept. Who knows what adventure God has planned for us, eh?"

"That's right," said Ari. "Now, though, let's go and meet our friend. I think you'll like Gusta, Nicolas." She got to her feet. "Come on," she said, "I'll buy you a coffee."

THE END

Ago Glain (Crab with peanut sauce)

Ingredients

6 large fresh crabs,
about 1 ½ lbs.
3 large tomatoes
1 sprig of parsley, chopped
3 large onion, 2 chopped
Juice of 3 limes
1 tbs. minced chilies

1 c. vinegar
2 c. peanut butter
1 bay leaf

3 whole cloves
1 tbs. palm oil
Salt and pepper to
taste

Directions

1. Place crabs in a large pot full of boiling water; add vinegar.
2. Season with salt and pepper and cook for 10 mins., skimming off any foam that forms on the surface of the water.
3. Add whole tomatoes, bay leaf, parsley and the whole onion with the cloves stuck into it.

4. Continue cooking for 5 mins., then remove the tomatoes and continue cooking the other ingredients for another 5 mins.
5. Remove the crabs, remove their shells and take out the crab meat from the body and the claws.
6. Mix the crab meat with the lime juice and set aside.
7. Heat the palm oil in a pan and add the finely chopped onion and fry until translucent.
8. Add the tomatoes and peanut butter and cook until they form a paste; add chilies.
9. Add crab meat and stir to heat through.
10. Stuff the crab meat into the cleaned shells and serve with rice; garnish with parsley.

Spicy Yam Soup

Ingredients

1 lb. chicken, cut into bite-sized chunks

1 large sweet potato, peeled and diced

1 clove garlic, minced

4 c. chicken broth

1 tsp. thyme

2 tbs. creamy peanut butter

½ tsp. ground cumin

1 small onion, chopped

1 cup chunky salsa

15 oz. can garbanzo beans, drained

1 c. diced zucchini

½ c. cooked rice

Directions

1. Heat the oil in a stockpot over medium heat; sauté onion, chicken, sweet potato and garlic until onion is soft. Turn down heat to prevent burning

2. Stir in broth, thyme and cumin; bring to boil, cover and simmer for about 15 mins.

3. Stir in salsa, garbanzo beans and zucchini; simmer for about 15 mins., until tender.

4. Stir in cooked rice and peanut butter, until the peanut butter dissolves.

5. Serve with pita bread or corn chips.

 Like the famous Cat, Mark Adderley was born in Cheshire, England. His early influences included C. S. Lewis and adventure books of various kinds, and his teacher once wrote on his report card, "He should go in for being an author," advice that stuck with him. He studied for some years at the University of Wales, where he became interested in medieval literature, particularly the legend of King Arthur. But it was in graduate school that he met a clever and beautiful American woman, whom he moved to the United States to marry. He has been teaching writing and literature in America ever since, and is now the director of the Via Nova Catholic Education Program and a baker for Loafers Bakery in Yankton, South Dakota. He is the author of a number of novels about King Arthur for adults, and originally wrote the McCracken books for his younger two children.

66758548R00121

Made in the USA
Lexington, KY
23 August 2017